Also by Adam L. Penenberg:

Fiction

Virtually True
A dystopian techno-thriller

Non-fiction

Blood Highways
*The True Story behind the Ford-Firestone
Killing Machine*

Viral Loop
*From Facebook to Twitter, How Today's Smartest
Businesses Grow Themselves*

Spooked
(with Marc Barry)
Espionage in Corporate America

TRIAL & TERROR

ADAM L. PENENBERG

WAYZGOOSE PRESS

Published in the United States by Wayzgoose Press.

Edited by Dorothy Zemach.
Cover design by DJ Rogers.
Book design by Maureen Cutajar.

ISBN 13: 978-1-938757-02-0
ISBN 10: 1938757025

For the Penengirls:
Charlotte, Lila, & Sophie

TRIAL & TERROR

PROLOGUE

HAROLD GUNDY HEAVED INTO THE RAILING of his second-floor loft, splintering the wood and jack-knifing over. He flopped in mid-air, his pants bunched around his ankles, twisting and bellowing until he crashed into a glass coffee table below.

Sinatra's "Fly Me to the Moon" blared over the stereo, almost drowning out the steps of the intruder scrambling down the staircase. Gundy groaned as he slid on his belly over the shards, pinning a set of police crime photos underneath him. Blood trickled from a gash on his cheek. His eyes—eyes that could, depending on his needs, stare down an unruly witness on the stand or seduce a jury—were clouded with tears.

"Please," he gasped. "Call an ambulance."

His assailant readjusted a brown wig and stood, staring, gun in hand.

Gundy coughed, spraying blood. His arm was twisted under him, his shoulder oddly torqued. Glass fragments riddled his torso.

"Call a...fuck...fucking ambulance."

The intruder inched away until startled by a liquor cabinet.

"You'll fry for this." Gundy crawled toward his cell phone, which had been sitting on the now-shattered table, dragging several photos with him and smearing blood on the carpet. The pictures, black and white, were of a man shot through the head and hugged by a chalk outline. Gundy snatched the phone. The top of his head glistened. Blinded by tears, he relied on touch to locate the nine. Then found the one.

"Stop." Gundy's assailant stepped forward.

Gundy regarded the gun, cocked and ready to fire. "Sh-sh-shoot. The cops...trace it."

Before he could punch in the final digit, Gundy dropped the phone and clutched his heart. He rolled onto his stomach and fell into sobs and a breathy mantra, "Sorry, sorry, sorry," until he abruptly cut off.

Gundy lay still, his eyes open and empty. The intruder approached cautiously and, finding no pulse, left to rummage through the liquor cabinet, where bottles of absinthe, bourbon, and gin were lined up in rows; and as the next song kicked off with a swinging intro, Sinatra swearing "It Had To Be You," seized a bottle of mescal.

Gundy's attacker hit him, then again, and again, until the bottle shattered his skull. Blood and mescal puddled together. A digital clock flipped to 10:21 p.m. As Sinatra and the band swung to the end, the killer yanked up Gundy's shirt tails, exposing a back marked with accordion folds of fat, took hold of a tube of lipstick, and began to draw.

PART I

SHADOW

CHAPTER 1

SUMMER NEUWIRTH SAT AT THE defense table, flipping through her State Law Handbook, letting her eyes glaze over the legal jargon and strings of penal code numbers. She tried to block out the stares of her client, Shadow Marsalis, who was perched forty-five degrees in his chair, his eyes glued to her profile.

Nearby, she heard whispering. "I've seen more trials than you've seen ball games," Ed Sprague, a bailiff for twenty years, said to Gus Patterson, a new recruit. "This one's going to do some serious time."

Patterson put his moustache comb back in its case. Growing a moustache was a rite of passage for Haze County bailiffs. "No way. He's getting off."

Sprague guffawed. "He already got off. That's why he's here."

Summer eyed the bailiffs. Patterson looked away. Sprague ogled her legs, until he noticed her noticing him. Too weary to be disgusted, Summer turned her attention back to the legal handbook, to the page on crimes of moral turpitude.

But she wasn't reading; she was thinking. Summer's nerves had been frayed even before she'd been assigned this case. Harold Gundy, the prosecutor, had used it not only to advance his political career but also to torment her. After opening arguments, he'd trapped her in an elevator and asked, "How do you know you're not defending *your* rapist? How do you know *he* isn't the one who burned your back and tortured you?"

Then there was the day Leah Davenport, the victim, had to be restrained when the video of her rape was played for the jury. Afterward, she caught up with Summer in the hall, wouldn't let her escape. Sobbing, she said, "Underneath your law degree you're a woman. Just like me. And as a woman, how can you defend this maniac? How can you live with yourself?"

The words echoed in Summer's head.

"They don't like you," Marsalis said, interrupting her thoughts.

Summer kept her eyes on the printed page. "They don't like what I do, which is to provide you with the best legal counsel possible."

Marsalis gripped her hand. "I like you."

Summer slid her hand out from under his and closed the handbook. "Cut it out."

"You're a beautiful woman."

Summer kept her eyes forward. She considered showing Marsalis the laminated photo of herself standing by a toothy man and two children she kept stashed in her wallet. All unmarried female public defenders carried the same snapshot.

They had chipped in to hire a model and kids so they could tell their more twisted clients—the sickos, pervs, and sex maniacs that made up the majority of their caseloads—they were married, not that it usually mattered.

Marsalis didn't pursue it. "What if Gundy doesn't show?" he asked.

"If a district attorney can't be at the reading of a verdict, a substitute D.A. can take his place," Summer said. "Happens all the time. All of us—the judges, D.A.s, public defenders—have huge case loads and often start another trial right after closing arguments."

"*He* doesn't appear busy." Marsalis pointed a crooked finger at the Honorable Judge Morton Hightower, lazing in his chambers, the door ajar. The judge wore snakeskin cowboy boots, which he propped up on his polished oak desk as he poked at an iPad. A game, judging by his demeanor.

Summer shrugged. She decided not to tell Marsalis that Hightower held the record for the most death row sentences— thirteen, immortalized in a collage of mug shots pinned to his desk by a sheet of glass.

She couldn't wait to get the verdict over with, so she could put Marsalis behind her. He was a man who shunned sunlight, an information broker who earned his keep cracking computer systems, tracking down precious data and selling to the highest bidder.

Marsalis had been arrested after Davenport brought the police a DVD showing him raping her. She claimed Marsalis had become infatuated with her after infiltrating her email. He'd stalked her at school, turning up in odd places and at odd times. At first, she'd thought he was harmless, but one night he broke into her room and attacked. Later, he mailed her the video.

Looking at Marsalis now, Summer couldn't imagine this small, insignificant geek as the man who had brutalized Davenport.

An open-and-shut case for the D.A. But although Davenport told the police she had been tied up during her ordeal, the rope didn't show up on the video. Summer subpoenaed Davenport's phone records and discovered that the "alleged victim," which is how Summer referred to her throughout the trial, had called him three, four times daily before and after the rape. When Davenport took the stand and denied ever having called Marsalis, Summer, on cross-examination, destroyed her credibility.

To escape Marsalis's prying eyes, Summer walked over to Sprague. "Did you try him at home?"

Sprague's expression was like, *Don't tell me my job.*

Before he could say anything, the judge called out, "Eddie, give Harold another try at home."

"Yes, sir." Sprague punched the numbers—by heart this time—and mumbled, "I've called five times already."

He held the phone to Summer's ear: ringing, followed by a curt voice message greeting.

"I've never known Harold not to call if he was going to miss a verdict," Sprague said. "Maybe there was a mix up."

Summer nodded. "The district attorney's office is sending over a proxy?"

"Sidney Raines. Should be here any minute."

Gundy's top assistant and heir-apparent. The last time Summer had tangled with him she'd been representing a third-strike crack-head arrested for stealing two slices of pizza. Raines had refused to plea to a misdemeanor, so her client got the max: twenty-five-to-life. After sentencing, for the benefit of a *Haze County Register* reporter, Raines made quite a show of praying for her client's soul.

Raines huffed through the court's padded doors, prompting the judge to place his iPad on his desk and enter the court. Sprague didn't wait for the judge's order to bring the jury in. Davenport, a dance student at the University, and her supporters—parents and a group of blue jean and chino-clad classmates—filed in from the hall.

Summer's nerves jangled. She always tensed before the reading of a verdict. The jurors settled into their chairs, avoiding Marsalis's probing eyes. When everyone was in place, the judge asked the jury foreman, "Has the jury reached a verdict?"

The foreman was someone Summer would have excluded if she hadn't run out of peremptory challenges: Walter Davies, a gun shop owner. Things didn't look bright for Marsalis.

Davies cleared his throat. "Yes, Your Honor."

Marsalis stopped probing the jury with his eyes and turned his attention back to Summer. He leaned in close to her, hand cupped to his mouth in classic client-attorney style. "Do you love me?"

Summer's spine stiffened. Usually the reading of verdict was enough to suck the ardor out of anyone. "Mr. Marsalis, the charges against you are serious."

"Do you, do you love me? *Answer me!*" Marsalis raged the last two words. The whole courtroom turned toward the disturbance.

Summer tried to ignore the eyes focused on her. "Stop it," she mouthed.

"Tell me!"

She hissed, "*No.*"

The foreman handed a square of paper to Sprague, who

carried it to the judge. Hightower unfolded the origami and read it to himself—Summer searched his expression for a hint, but Hightower didn't provide any.

Marsalis bit his bottom lip until it bleached white; then, his face displaying rank ecstasy, unfurled a skein of numbers in her ear.

Summer tried to concentrate on the proceedings.

Marsalis rambled on. "Four-two-two-five-oh-one-one-four..."

It took Summer a moment to realize he was reciting her Visa card number.

"Ms. Neuwirth, is anything the matter?" the judge asked.

"Oh-eight-three-six..." Marsalis also had her social security number.

Nothing Summer could do now. "No, no, Your Honor."

The judge didn't press. Abnormal behavior was the norm in the criminal justice system. "Well, then, will the defendant rise?"

Summer and Marsalis stood. She noticed her hands were shaking; her heart was beating against her ribs; sweat chilled her back.

Marsalis squeezed her pinky. Summer stayed shocked-still. "Twelve-seven-fifty-three," he whispered. "Really, Summer, using your mother's birth date as your pin number? It took me no time to crack."

Summer wanted to run. She didn't need more nightmares; since her own rape, she had already suffered more than her fair share.

"Oh, ooh, ooh," Marsalis whispered in an orgasmic coo. "And $26,142 in law school debt? Tsk tsk tsk, Summer. Perhaps it would have been more prudent to accept that job with

Brockton, Myers & Bellamy. They offered a much more attractive financial package than the Haze County Public Defenders Office."

The judge was speaking: "...case number 62-8702, the state versus Eugene Robert Marsalis, on the charge of rape and assault in the first degree—"

Marsalis released Summer's pinky. He stood ramrod-straight.

"We find the defendant—"

Summer gripped the table and shut her eyes.

"—*not* guilty."

Summer sank into her chair. The rest of Judge Hightower's words were covered by a carpet of courtroom hisses and calls for justice. Summer glanced at Davenport, who was sobbing.

It was the verdict Summer had sought, but all she could feel now was crushing regret.

Raines splatted his briefcase on the table, refusing to look at the jury. On his way out he brushed past Summer. "You'll be sorry you got this pond scum off."

Summer was already sorry.

Davenport, her eyes red and haunted, approached. Marsalis had already skulked out of the courtroom and was, Summer hoped, out of her life.

"I never called him. That was a bunch of lies." Davenport sought answers in Summer's eyes but broke down before she could get any.

Summer left her and rushed into the hallway. Eyes fixed on floor squares the whole way, she slipped into the women's bathroom.

She filled a sink, pressed the soap dispenser, and tried to cleanse herself. The walls were dingy and yellowed. The stench of cleanser barely masked other odors. She stared at her reflection in the mirror; backlit by the uneven fluorescent glare, she looked ravaged and haggard.

Through the mirror Summer saw Marsalis step inside. Startled, she gripped the sink and spoke to his reflection. "Get out."

Marsalis squeezed a flat-line smile and stepped forward.

Refusing to give in to her fear, Summer turned to face him. "What do you want from me? I got you acquitted."

"You did not get me acquitted, I got me acquitted," Marsalis said, his tone a model of controlled menace. "If I hadn't been able to enter the telephone company's database and alter her phone records, I would not be a free man. All of my hard work would have been for naught."

Summer searched for a way out.

Marsalis poised himself between her and the door. "You have no idea who you are dealing with."

He inched closer. Summer backed away until she was pressed against the wall.

Marsalis clamped a hand around her arm, found a pressure point, and squeezed. Summer's knees buckled. When she flailed, he gripped her tighter, and with his other hand, pushed his thumb into her clavicle until she was on her knees.

"Let me tell you about mosquitoes," he said. "When one attaches itself to my arm, I don't crush it, I torment it. I flex my arm and it's trapped by its stinger. But it keeps sucking blood, gorging on it. It can't stop. Until *pop!*" His breath was hot on her face.

Summer gasped. "You're hurting me."

"This is true." He smiled again.

"I'll... I'll go to the police."

"And tell them the man you successfully defended for rape is out to get you? I think not. It's too early in your career to ruin your reputation."

The door swung open. When the woman spotted Marsalis, she uttered a choked sound and fled.

"Security will be here in a few seconds," Summer said.

Marsalis released his grip, leaving her sprawled on the tile. "I will leave you with one more piece of information," Marsalis said. "Harold Gundy, born on June 29th, 1948, at 6:43 a.m. at Haze County General Hospital, died a little before 10:21 last night."

Marsalis bent over and kissed her cheek, tenderly. "I'll be in touch, Summer."

CHAPTER 2

WHILE HAZE COUNTY'S DISTRICT ATTORNEYS worked in sparkling digs, public defenders were crowded into a sighing edifice across the boulevard. Punishment for doing their jobs. Although the county was bankrupt, the legislature voted pay raises for the D.A.s, while the P.D.s staggered through a two-year salary and hiring freeze. Twice a week, the A/C shorted out, like today, office cynicism rising with the temperature.

District attorneys dared to dream of plum assignments on federally funded task forces on drugs, gangs, and sex crimes, where the hours were shorter and the caseloads lighter. After putting in their time, they could then vie for judgeships or political office. But public defenders' careers ended where they started. Never in the county's history had a public defender been elected a judge or to Congress. They were sentenced to forever work in the twisted realm of the psychotic.

And because of the company they kept, P.D.s were universally despised—by the judges, the D.A.s, the public; and, because they were usually the bearers of bad news, even their clients.

Summer slid her ID card into an electronic lock and opened a frosted glass door: *Haze County Public Defenders Office.* She breezed down cramped aisles, smiling and issuing silent hellos to the paralegals and receptionists.

It was an hour after the verdict had been read, and she was calm. She had filed away Marsalis in an isolated part of her mind, and this enabled her to function. All public defenders acquired this skill; if you didn't, you wouldn't last. Like her father, a homicide detective who had worked the other side of the criminal justice system, had taught her. Got the flu? Suck down some vitamin C and get back to work. Depressed? Stop feeling sorry for yourself. Got menstrual cramps during closing arguments? Walk it off. Because when others depend on you, there are no excuses.

Summer headed to the conference room, where her boss, Jon Levi, and her BFF, Rosie Aridjis, were chatting over lunch.

Levi was gesturing with his hands. "...waiting for the light to change. If I'm late again Judge Landburgh's going to serve my scrotum on a plate. So I sprint across even though the light was red. I figure I'm in the clear until a cop pulls me over. I just about spew my lunch: Patrolman Samuel Hoeg. I'd skewered him on cross like a week ago. I figure just to get back at me he's going to throw me in the slammer. I mean, for jay-fuckin'-walkin'?"

Rosie was painting her fingernails maroon to match her toes. Her arms were scarred from the removal of gang tattoos. "They love doing shit like that to Latinos," she said, not looking up from her brush. "Just to fuck with us."

When they caught sight of Summer, they applauded.

"Congrats on your first 'not guilty,'" Levi said.

Summer bowed her head a smidge. It had been a hollow victory, but it was a victory nevertheless.

"How'd Gundy take the agony of defeat?" Rosie asked.

Summer flipped her lunch bag on the table, next to some mail. She picked up the stack of post-its and envelopes and peeked under the rubber band. "Señor Gundy didn't show, so Raines did the honors." She turned to Rosie. "Did that new secretary give you my mail again?"

Rosie nodded with sarcastic eyes. "He can't remember who's who."

"Actually," Levi reflected, "except for the hair and Rosie's nightmarish taste in clothes, you could be sisters."

Rosie sputtered. "My taste in clothes? Look at you, dressed like some acid-popping hairy-legged commune-dwelling"— she turned sweet when Levi raised an eyebrow—"first class legal mind. It is an honor, an honor I say, to serve under you."

"Duly noted," Levi said. "Sure not like Gundy to miss a rape verdict."

Summer shrugged. "What happened with Hoeg?"

"Oh, yeah. So I'm wearing this Jerry Garcia tie and the same suit I wore to this party a few days ago, and I—shut up, Rosie."

Rosie's neon-charged smile caused her to trap a hair in the crook of her mouth. Because her nails were wet, she couldn't get to it. She tried spitting it out. Summer pulled it free. "Thanks. I didn't say anything, Jon."

"You didn't have to. Anyway, I remember I have this joint in my pocket. I could see the *Haze County Register* headlines: 'County's Chief Public Defender Arrested for Drugs.'"

"So," Rosie asked, "you do some kung-fu action upside his head? Or did you beg?"

"I begged. 'Please officer, I'm late to court. No hard feelings because I questioned your manhood on the stand, blah blah blah.' He let me go with a warning."

"Close call." Summer unwrapped her sandwich. "Good thing they don't drug test public defenders. If they did, there wouldn't be any."

Rosie blew on her nails. "You know, the cops who get all righteous over traffic laws are usually the ones who shake down dealers and then re-sell their shit on the street."

"Well," Levi said, turning to Summer, "enlighten us, oh victorious one. How'd you manage to win an acquittal in a case where the cops had a fucking video of the crime in progress?"

Summer reached down to pick her napkin off the floor. "Davenport's phone records show she phoned my client a bunch of times before and after the incident. She took the stand and denied it."

"Awesome!"

"I hated it, Jon. My client was… " Summer paused, unsure how much to reveal. "I've never had a case where I knew the guy was guilty and a threat to public safety and still got him off."

"That's because you never won before," Rosie said.

"Nobody wins around here," Levi said. "Hell, it took me six years before I won one, and that was in the days when the State Supreme Court was liberal and the legislature hadn't gotten into the act. Back then, you had a fighting chance. Now it's just one big funnel to convict. But what do I always tell you guys?"

Summer and Rosie said in unison, "Don't get caught up personally with clients or the case. Just provide the best possible defense counsel possible."

They laughed as Levi offered mock applause. "If you have a picture of the guy, I could pass it out to the bailiffs, make sure he doesn't show up here or in court," he said.

Summer considered it, but no. Marsalis was right. After getting him off, there was no way Summer could ask for protection. "I'll be all right."

"Want me to get some of my, uh, associates to kick his ass?" Rosie often defended old acquaintances from the 'hood.

"Do you have pics of the alleged rapee?" Levi asked.

Summer rummaged through her briefcase and showed them a xeroxed photo of Davenport.

Levi whistled. "I'd do her."

Rosie squinted. "Shit. I'd do her, too."

P.D. lore: The chances of winning acquittal in a rape case diminish with the attractiveness of the victim.

Summer pushed her sandwich away and stood up to stretch. "I'm still recovering from Tuesday's closing arguments. My butt fell asleep."

"Gundy does go on," Rosie said. "Whenever I go *mujer-a-mano* with Gundy I'm tempted to bring my ben-wa balls to court. Give myself something to do until he stops talking—or I find a boyfriend—whichever comes first."

"When you object, you'd better stay seated," Summer said. "Anyway, I thought you had a boyfriend."

"We broke up."

"Sorry."

"Don't be."

Levi broke in. "Speaking of Gundy, did you hear? Jack Brauer got out of county psych last week." Noting Summer and Rosie's blank expressions, he clarified. "I guess that was before your time. About what, eight years ago, this pro-life artichoke shot Jonathan Sadbury, an abortion doc, in the head, right outside his clinic. Gundy, as you know, is pro-life himself—"

"Except when he's prosecuting one of our clients," Summer interrupted.

"—And he let Brauer plead not guilty by reason of insanity and had him committed. Now Brauer's free."

"I remember this," Summer said. "His wife was that feminist who goes by initials, SK."

"Right. When Gundy let Brauer cop an insanity plea, SK said the minute Brauer got out she'd hunt Gundy down and blow him away."

"It'd sure save us a lot of grief if she made good on it." Rosie poured soda into her mouth without letting the can touch her lips.

"They never give insanity to *us*, only when they know they'll score political points." Summer sat down and picked at the remnants of her sandwich.

Rosie rested her head on the cool of the conference table. "Man, I think the nail polish got me high."

"Don't let Officer Hoeg hear you." Levi tapped Summer on the shoulder. "At least Marsalis is out of your hair."

"I hope so," Summer said, nibbling on leftover sandwich bits. "He's a computer hacker. Today, during the reading of the verdict, he greeted me with my financial records."

"Guess he wanted to ensure primo service," Rosie said.

Levi dished the remains of his potato salad into the trash. "Spooky. But hell, we make so little money, what harm could he do?"

Summer rubbed her eyes. "I am so sorry I got him off."

Levi tucked his Tupperware into his briefcase. "Think of it this way: He makes up for some of the innocent clients who are convicted."

Rosie perked her head up. "Yeah, all one of them."

Outside Summer's office, Rosie had tacked up a Not Guilty banner, which would stay up until someone else got a client off. Could be a while. Summer leafed through her mail and checked her voicemail—the usual junk, clients demanding action, D.A.s demanding discovery evidence, P.D.s from other cities demanding information on ex-clients.

The last message was from Eddie of Brockton, Myers & Bellamy, a glitzy firm specializing in defending pimps, drug dealers, and prostitutes. The only difference between their clients and Summer's was that theirs earned a better living breaking the law and could afford private attorneys. Every few months Brockton called to offer Summer a position; but not, she knew, because she was a good attorney. To Brockton, she would always be just a nice-looking piece of furniture. Summer crumpled up the note, but then after thinking about it, smoothed it out and dropped it in her purse.

On her way out, Summer passed Levi's office. He motioned for her to come in. "I know I said this already, but nice work on the video-rape trial. You've come a long way."

"Thanks." Summer checked her watch.

"What are you working on next?"

"Off to Court Nine to pick up a new client. His name is Jimi Cruz."

"What'd he do? *Allegedly.*" Levi smirked.

"Petty theft at Neiman Marcus that turned into a felony-stupid when he assaulted a security guard. Until today, I didn't know you could commit petty theft at Neiman Marcus."

"Hope he's better behaved than your last."

Summer shrugged. "How about you?"

Levi rolled down his sleeves. "After the verdict comes in on my capital case, I'm restarting jury selection for a molestation case. The judge wiped out the first batch with one question: *Have any of you been molested or know someone who's been molested?* No shit. Sixty hands went up."

Levi gathered up his briefcase and walked with Summer to the elevator, cackling the whole way.

He didn't notice Summer wasn't laughing.

CHAPTER 3

COURT NINE WAS WHERE ARRAIGNMENTS were held. In a wire cage were about two dozen handcuffed men and a smattering of women, mostly hookers and dope shaggers. They were flanked by bailiffs. When Summer passed the cage, prisoners stomped, whistled, and made kissy noises.

Summer didn't look. She relied on the same steely resolve she used whenever she came here. She sat in the visitors' gallery, in a section reserved for attorneys, and could almost hear her father's words: *Don't let them get to you. Don't ever show weakness.* He had been talking about himself, his experiences as a cop; but for her, the same rules applied.

She only had to wait a few minutes before Jimi Cruz's name was called. A bailiff plucked a rangy kid out of the cage and stood him in front of the judge. His hair was matted in what were once-blond dreadlocks. He had dozens of tattoos—chains and snakes mostly—and piercings: rings and studs in his nose, eyebrow, earlobes, lip, and probably in places Summer didn't care to know about.

He was a member of the gutter tribes—suburban kids who came to the city to panhandle, sleep on the streets, and shoot heroin. Cruz wore a ripped tank top that, while once white, was now grimy puke. On his skin, where tattoos ended, filth began.

"I'm your lawyer. Summer Neuwirth." She handed him a business card.

Cruz smiled, showing bad teeth. "I know. Been here before."

The arraignment judge, William Angiers, was second-generation Haze County judiciary. But while his father had clawed his way to a seat on the State Supreme Court, Angiers, because of a well-publicized drinking problem, was trapped here. Levi had warned Summer about Angiers her first day: *Don't talk back. He's tough but fair, his wrath displayed in direct proportion to the degree of his hangover.*

But where was the district attorney? Although the D.A.'s office was notorious for bungling paperwork, no one ever missed an arraignment. Unless there was a mix up—or a crisis. First Gundy, now this. Summer wondered what was going on.

Angiers shuffled through the pile of folders spread over his desk. "Cruz, Cruz," he muttered. He looked over at his court clerk. "Where's the file on Cruz?"

The clerk searched through an even bigger pile, then shrugged.

Angiers removed his eyeglasses, rubbed his eyes, and peered over his gavel. His face was even puffier than usual. Summer was struck by how labored his breathing was. "And where is the D.A.?"

Summer, the clerk, the judge, and Cruz all scoured the courtroom, but came up empty.

Angiers made a show of containing his anger. Then he turned to Cruz and growled, "Not in any hurry, are you, young man?"

Cruz shook his head. "No, Your Honor. I'm very sorry the court has to take the time to locate my file. It must be frustrating to have to deal with bureaucracy on a day-to-day basis."

Angiers leaned forward, rested his elbow on the desk, propping his chin up with his hand, his attitude like, *Wow, it can talk!* "You went to college?"

"Yes, sir. Two years at Wesleyan University."

"You dropped out?"

Cruz nodded.

"Drugs?"

"Heroin."

Summer glanced at Cruz's track-marked arm. He lived in a world of needles—from piercings to tattoos to heroin—pain and pleasure and image inextricably bound. The result was a generation of needle addicts, addicted to the needle as much as to the drug.

Angiers eyed his clerk, who was now rifling through the files piled next to the judge. He snapped at her: "I already looked through those. Listen, find me a D.A. so we can clear up these cases. And call the police, see if they sent over this young man's reports. I don't even know what he's been charged with."

Cruz was rocking back and forth on his feet. "I was hungry, so I shoplifted a box of gourmet cookies, Your Honor. When the security guard grabbed me, I slugged him."

Summer wanted to slug Cruz. Although Angiers seemed pleased with his honesty, there went any plea bargain. She said, "Let me do the talking for you, Jimi. You'll just get yourself in more hot water."

Through the courtroom doors, a bailiff rushed in, sweaty and breathless. "Permission to approach the bench," he said.

Angiers reveled in his testiness. "Not unless you can magically transform yourself into a district attorney. You know I do not like my court disrupted, Sal. Before I let you approach, I want my overpaid clerk to tell me where Mr. Cruz's file is."

Sal scratched his arm. "It's an emergency, Your Honor."

Angiers slammed down his mug, spilling coffee on his wrist. The clerk handed him napkins and Angiers mopped up the mess. "Oh, all right. What is it?"

The bailiff climbed behind the bench and whispered in the judge's ear. Angiers's face blanched. He whispered back. When the bailiff nodded, Angiers's head drooped. "Thank you, Sal," he whispered. "I'm sorry I gave you a hard time."

It took Angiers a few restless moments before he got back to Cruz. He removed his glasses, clenching them in his hand. Summer could see tears bunching in his eyes. "Young man, I wake up every morning wondering why I should cut anyone a break. Do you know what answer I come up with?"

"No, sir."

"In the hopes they never end up in front of me in court ever again." Angiers pointed to a wall of photos behind him, more than a hundred of them, neatly arranged. "These are portraits of people with whom I cut a deal. The few covered with yellow stickies were those foolish enough to get in trouble with the law again, and they are now very sorry they did. Do you understand?"

Cruz nodded.

Angiers itched his scalp. "I view them as personal failures. And failure does not sit well with me. Do you promise you will never show your face around my court again?"

"Yes, sir."

"Do you swear to me you will seek treatment for your drug problem?"

"Yeah, Judge. You have my word."

"I'm not sure what that's worth. Approach the bench, Mr. Cruz."

First the file, then the D.A. a no-show. Today was Cruz's lucky day. Usually, Angiers gave this speech only when the holding tank was about to bust open. Cruz ambled forward. The clerk dusted off the camera. Summer averted her eyes to avoid the flash and caught sight of Rosie.

Rosie mouthed: *I have to talk to you.*

Summer held up a finger: *Wait a sec.*

"Ms. Neuwirth!" Angiers shouted.

Summer jumped through her skin. "Yes, Your Honor?"

"Explain to your client what has transpired. Give him the names of drug rehabilitation programs. Make sure you get the message across. Now, get him out of here before I change my mind."

"Yes, Judge Angiers. I will. And thank you."

"Thank you," Cruz chimed in, bowing.

As the clerk printed out the photo and stuck it up with the rest, Angiers adjourned for the day.

Summer led Cruz to a side room where they sat catty-corner at a tiny broken desk, her back to the door. Too close for Summer's comfort. There was always the possibility of contracting TB from clients, especially those who lived on the street.

He had said he'd been here before. That meant he probably had at least one prior conviction, if not two. If he had two felony convictions, two strikes against him, then the judge had made a crucial error. If they found Cruz's file, the police could drag him back.

"Thanks for your help." Cruz was shaking.

"I didn't do anything."

"Well, um, thanks for being here. The last few times—"

"I've been instructed by the court to provide you with the names of drug rehabilitation facilities."

"Tried that already. No slots available."

Summer knew this. Although the federal government was willing to spend hundreds of millions on drug interdiction and border patrols, there was no political will to provide users with tools to escape their addictions. If Cruz stuck around Haze County, it was only a matter of time before he'd end up serving hard time.

She looked around, and then whispered, "The weather in Costa Rica is wonderful this time of year."

"What?"

Summer couldn't *tell* him to flee—she could be charged with aiding and abetting a felon. "The weather in Haze County, for you, could get very hot, very uncomfortable. Wouldn't you like to get away from it all? Go to Las Vegas or New York or Dallas?"

"A vacation?"

"Far away from here."

"How far?"

"Far."

Cruz cracked a grin and scratched an armpit. "You know, I've always wanted to see Vegas."

"I hear it's so brightly lit, you can get a tan at midnight."

"Thanks," Cruz said. "I owe you one."

"No offense, Mr. Cruz, but the best payback is if I never see you again."

Cruz wiped his nose with the bottom of his tank top, displaying a belly button stud and a tattoo of a syringe, the needle squirting dots of liquid. He stood, his giggling muffled by his shirt, and left.

Skirting the law made Summer nervous, although it beat letting Cruz get twenty-five-to-life for stealing cookies. She hoped he had the sense to leave the state before seeking his next fix.

A buzzing noise from inside her purse. She reached in to pull out her phone. Eddie Brockton calling again. She stared at the number. OK, so he was a sleaze. But what would it be like to work in a glittering office tower, representing freshly scrubbed clients in designer suits and silk dresses, to pick and choose clients instead of being picked on and chosen, to earn five times the money with one-tenth the stress? Cruz wasn't the only one who could escape.

She jammed the phone back in her purse while mentally composing her resignation letter to the P.D.'s office:

> *Dear Jon,*
>
> *I just can't take it any more. I suffer fighter-pilot fear every time I walk down a deserted street or turn a corner at night alone, afraid a former client is going to beat me, or rape me, or kill me. Just getting through the workday is a personal triumph.*
>
> *It shouldn't be like this. I'm going where the money is. I'm going where the living is easy.*
>
> *After what I've been through, I hope you'll forgive me. I did my best.*

She was jarred by a hand on her shoulder.

It was Rosie: "Gundy's dead. I just heard the cops found him. He was murdered. Some weird, twisted serial thing."

"What?" Summer stuffed the note back in her purse.

"You think it could've been your psycho video-rapist?"

Summer thought of her run-in with Marsalis in the bathroom. "He had no reason to kill Gundy," she said carefully. "He won."

"Gundy got it the night before the verdict. Marsalis couldn't have known he was going to get off."

"What was the time of death?"

"Don't know. Why?"

"Something he said." Summer shivered.

Rosie tapped out a cigarette from a pack of Lucky Strikes. There was no smoking in court buildings, so she jabbed it, unlit, into her mouth. "If the cops want to talk to you, what are you going to say?"

"I'll claim attorney-client confidentiality. But you know, I don't think Marsalis did it."

"Shit. Maybe you're right. Hell. You, me, all P.D.s had better reasons to ice that bastard than Marsalis did."

CHAPTER 4

SUMMER WAS BACK IN HIGHTOWER'S COURT. This time as a defendant.

She glanced over to Jimi Cruz, his lips purple and crusty, handcuffed and wrapped in a jumpsuit, *Haze County Jail* emblazoned on the back. He was spitting air, trying to get her attention, but she knew better than to make eye contact.

She couldn't help herself. "How bad is it?"

Levi looked away. "Can't say until I've cross-examined Cruz."

"But Raines wouldn't have initiated this if he didn't think he could nail me, right?"

Levi leaned closer, whispered. "You know better than to ask that. Summer, you're a terrific attorney, but a lousy client. Bragg is right behind us, so shut up and look innocent."

Summer resisted the urge to peek back at Chuck Bragg, court reporter for the *Haze County Register*, who sat a couple of rows back, a spiral-bound notebook poised on his lap.

Raines addressed the judge. "The charges against Ms. Neuwirth are serious. She knew Mr. Cruz had two strikes against him, yet she encouraged him to flee the state. It's all in the police report."

Levi scowled. "Objection. Sidney knows a police report is not admissible."

Hightower peered over his eyeglasses. "Jon, this is a hearing, not a trial; therefore, I will allow the inclusion of the police report. Go ahead, Sidney."

Raines paraphrased, "Officer Mobley was involved in a drug sweep. When Mr. Cruz offered to sell him heroin, the officer tried to arrest him. But Mr. Cruz threw the heroin in his face and fled. The officer gave chase, cornering him two blocks down. When he attempted to pacify the suspect, Cruz screamed, 'I have AIDS,' and bit him on the arm, drawing blood."

"Does he?" the judge asked.

"Thankfully, no."

The judge slid Cruz an oblique glance. "What did the ever-excitable Mr. Cruz do next?"

"The officer brought him downtown. In the van, Mr. Cruz said—"

Levi sprang to his feet. "Objection! Let's cut the hearsay. Mr. Cruz is right here."

Hightower reflected. "That sounds reasonable. But Eddie," he said to the advancing Sprague, who was never more than a half-step behind the judge, "don't unchain him. Leave him where he is." He turned to Cruz. "I must emphasize you are under oath. Continue, Sidney."

Raines stared Cruz down. "Do you remember the attorney assigned to you three days ago?"

Cruz grinned. "She's a babe, Sid."

"Could you identify her?"

"Sure. Blonde, blue-eyed—Hey, Summer, is that blouse teal or aqua?"

Summer tried not to smile.

Levi said, "We'll stipulate Ms. Neuwirth was Mr. Cruz's attorney."

"Thanks," Cruz said. "Nice tie, dude. Jerry lives." He clanked a shackled arm in the air.

Raines broke in. "When you and I met at police headquarters, what did you tell me with regards to your attorney's conduct?"

"She talked about the weather. I said Haze County is hot this time of year. It is. Dries out my skin. Do you have any idea how hard it is to find moisturizer when you're homeless?"

"What else did Ms. Neuwirth say?"

"She said I deserved a vacation."

"Did you tell her you had two strikes?"

Cruz eyed his chains and mumbled a stream of curses.

Raines took it in stride. "What did you say, Mr. Cruz?"

Cruz looked up, aiming hate at Raines, then looked beyond to Summer, his eyes brushing hers. She could tell Cruz was struggling with himself. But, with a sigh, he fell in line. "Yeah, I told her."

Summer's stomach twisted in on itself. This was bad.

"What did she say to you?" Raines asked.

"If I didn't want to spend twenty-five years in jail, I should get my sorry white ass out of state."

"I assume she didn't use the term 'sorry white ass.' " It pained Raines, a religious man, to say "ass."

"You assume right, old man."

"So the facts, as you remember them, are that you informed Ms. Neuwirth that you had two strikes, and she advised you to flee."

"If you say so."

"Do *you* say so?"

Cruz chewed imaginary cud. "Sure."

Raines turned to the judge. "I'm done with this witness, Your Honor."

Hightower nodded at Levi. "Your witness, Jon."

Levi approached, his hands jammed in his pockets. His jacket was crinkly and one of his socks was inside out. But what he lacked in sartorial sense, he made up for with legal presence. For the first time, Summer noticed that Levi's bald spot resembled a halo.

He sized up Cruz for a moment, and then plunged in. "If Ms. Neuwirth, as you allege, told you to leave the state, why did you stay?"

"I didn't have any money. Thought I'd unload some Mexican tar and hit the road."

"Were you under the influence of drugs at the time you first met Ms. Neuwirth?"

"Yup, but I'd come down by then."

"You were in jail for thirty-six hours prior to meeting Ms. Neuwirth. Is this correct?"

"Sounds about right."

"When do you usually begin to suffer the effects of withdrawal?"

"Put it this way," Cruz said, "I was seriously needing a fix when I faced that porky judge."

"Angiers," Levi clarified. "When you crave a fix, how is your memory?"

"I forget the question."

"That bad, huh?"

"When I need a fix I can barely remember to piss."

"Would you say it would be difficult to trust your memory?"

Cruz mimicked a British accent. "Damned foolhardy, if you ask me."

"Are you suffering withdrawal now, Mr. Cruz?"

"Nah," he said. "They put me on methadone, so I'm, like, with the program now."

Raines called out. "I object, Your Honor. Whether the witness is receiving treatment or not is irrelevant. Ms. Neuwirth's actions are at the crux of the matter."

"I am merely attempting to ascertain the reliability of the witness's memory," Levi said.

"That has no—"

"Hold on, Sidney." The judge held up his hand while scrolling Cruz's testimony on his computer monitor. He pursed his lips. "Sustained."

Levi's jaw plunged. "Your Honor?"

"I said *sustained*, Mr. Levi. If I follow the logic of your questioning, what you are implying is that Mr. Cruz's memory is better when he is under the influence of heroin than when he is not. This is not, nor ever will be, a compelling argument in my court. Now proceed."

Levi took a moment to collect his thoughts, then gestured to Raines. "Mr. Cruz, did the district attorney offer to wipe away your third strike in exchange for your testimony here today?"

"Objection!" Raines shouted.

Cruz shook his chains. "Fuckin' A, man. I would've never done it otherwise."

Raines continued. "I move the witness's last statement be stricken from the record."

"Oh, Sidney, what a crock," Levi said. "What did you offer this guy in exchange for his testimony? That he'd walk after a couple of years instead of twenty-five-to-life? For those terms you could get Gandhi to lie for you."

Raines shouted, overlapping Levi's remarks. "This is outrageous! How *dare* you—"

Hightower exploded, "*Order!* The next one who opens his mouth will be held in contempt!" The judge glanced at Bragg, then glared at Raines. "Sidney, what did you offer in exchange for Mr. Cruz's testimony?"

Raines made a show of controlling his temper. "My office agreed to drop the drug and assault charge and let him plea to a misdemeanor—six months jail time followed by six months community service and two years probation—for the Neiman's theft."

"You give a guy set to get twenty-five-to-life six months jail time?" Hightower waved his hand in front of his nose like he was clearing away a bad odor. Looking at Bragg, who was furiously scribbling notes, he said, "And the Register says judges are too eager to plea bargain?"

Cruz faked a sobbing fit. "I couldn't take it any more, Your Lordship. Commandant Raines said, 'Vee have vays ov making you talk,' and I cracked."

Hightower curled his lips. "Mr. Cruz, you are out of order!"

"Why, do I look broken?"

"Eddie," the judge said, "get Mr. Cruz out of my sight. I've heard quite enough from him."

After Cruz was gone, the judge sat with his hands folded. "Sidney, you know with this witness your case is difficult to prove.

I'm forced to recommend that the district attorney drop the charges." He leaned over the front of his bench, eyes on Summer. "However, Ms. Neuwirth, I am penning a letter of complaint to the American Bar Association. Just because there is not enough evidence for a trial doesn't mean I don't know you told him to skedaddle. Pull anything like that in my courtroom, you'll pay big time." Hightower smacked down his gavel. "Court dismissed!"

A slap on the wrist. It could have much worse. Summer hugged Levi.

"Somehow," Levi said, "I'm oddly aroused."

Summer kissed Levi's cheek and wiped away her own tear. "Thanks for everything, Jon."

"Wait till you get my bill."

Summer could hear Bragg breathing behind her.

Raines came over. "You caught a break today, Summer. But remember this: Keep bending the law, and I guarantee it'll snap back. At least the public won't have to deal with Mr. Cruz for a while."

Summer stumbled out of her seat. "You're not going to stick to your bargain?"

Raines fingered his lapel. "Recanting his testimony wasn't part of our bargain."

"Raines," she said, "you are one evil, cold-hearted son of a bitch."

"Easy, easy," Levi said, pulling Summer away. "Sidney, my office is going to ride shotgun for Cruz all the way to the Supreme Court if we have to. You know as well as I do that coercing a witness can get you disbarred."

Bragg said, "I can't write that fast. Summer, did you call Sidney an evil, cold-hearted bastard, or a son of a bitch?" The smile on his face said it all: *scoop!*

Raines pounded his fist into his palm to emphasize each point. "Bleeding heart liberals. Look at this guy's rap sheet. It's as long as my arm. Why shouldn't he stew in the pen for twenty-five years?"

"A deal is a deal and the law is the law," Summer said.

"What do you know about the law, sister?" Raines scoffed. "You think the penal code was designed to protect psychopaths like your video-rapist Marsalis or grubby parasites like Cruz?"

"I smell a vendetta, Sidney." Levi explained to Bragg, "The D.A. lost the Marsalis case, a case they should have won, so they concocted this scheme to discredit Ms. Neuwirth."

"That is complete, unadulterated"—Raines searched for the right words—"*dog poop!*" He frisbee'ed his briefcase across the floor.

" '*Dog poop*'?" Summer, Levi, and Bragg guffawed.

Levi maneuvered Summer out of the courtroom, away from Bragg and to a block of elevators. "Stay out of Hightower's court for a while," he said.

Summer thought of the resignation letter she had drafted the night before. But now wasn't the time. "What do you think will happen to Cruz?"

"Depends on what Bragg writes; depends on whether the mayor gets wind; depends on whether Raines is getting laid or not. Somehow I doubt he'll have to do major time. Who'd have thunk a specimen like Cruz would have a conscience? The least I can do is try my damndest for him."

They got into the elevator and Levi pushed 'L' for the lobby. "One more thing," he said as the doors hushed closed, "Gundy's funeral is tomorrow. I have to put in an appearance, but I advise you to stay away. No need to stir things up even more."

CHAPTER 5

R OSIE WANTED TO SPEND GUNDY'S FUNERAL at a bar owned by a former client she had once defended on a morals charge, but Summer wanted to stay in, cook, maybe watch a movie. That was many martinis ago. Now they were picking Chinese food out of cartons. The DVD was still in a plastic bag, on top of the TV.

"Then what happened?" Rosie wore black nail polish and even blacker lipstick. Her way of mourning for Gundy.

"Hightower told me I'd better watch myself in his court-room." Summer licked hoisin sauce off her fingers. "I'm lucky Cruz hates authority."

"You're luckier that gutter triber likes pretty girls." Rosie leaned back and lit a cigarette. "How are you getting on these days? You know, the, uh—"

Summer got up to open a window. "Rape? You can say it."

"Fine. I said it."

Air streamed in from the outside. "I feel guilty about rap-ing the poor guy, though he had it coming."

Rosie laughed, spilling martini on the floor. She soaked it up with a used napkin.

Summer looked out to the ocean, listening to the waves rumble.

"Are you still getting your head shrunk?" Rosie asked.

"I couldn't see the point," Summer said, "so I decided to work harder, give myself less time to think about it."

"Too close to home? I'm the same way. Mother trouble? Father failings?"

"Mother trouble." Summer settled at the table and took one of Rosie's cigarettes. She broke it in half, sprinkling crumbs. She weighed whether to let Rosie in on the turmoil that absorbed more and more of her thoughts: the rape, her mother's disappearance eight months ago, job stress, the fear that Marsalis would make good on his threats. Her reticence eroded by good gin, she started talking.

"From the time I could walk, my mother put rouge on my cheeks, painted my lips, stuck me in clingy dresses and tight pants, the same stuff she wore. She wouldn't even let me call her 'Mom.' It was always 'Sonia.' When I was in grammar school, she'd confide in me, tell me all about her affairs with movie stars, her sexual hang-ups, her unfulfilled dreams of stardom."

Rosie's eyes widened over her near-empty glass, but she didn't say anything. Summer knew Rosie wouldn't push because that would mean she'd have to talk about her father.

But Summer needed to tell someone. "It was like instead of being my mom, she wanted to be my best friend. You know, for months after the rape, I felt like I had somehow brought it on myself. But then I had this major epiphany one night when I couldn't sleep through the nightmares. It was all Sonia's fault.

She drilled into me the ways and means of beauty, taught me how to play the coquettish little whore, the charming schoolgirl, the mature woman. She showed me how to walk, how to flirt, how to trap a man, all before I was ten. Hell, if I did bring it on myself, then Sonia's the one who brought it on me."

"You know that's bullshit: No woman brings on her own rape," Rosie said. "You still get flashbacks? Ever scared?"

Summer held up her house keys, jangled them. Five just to get in her front door.

Rosie licked the rim of her glass. "Any word on the search for Sonia?"

"I don't think anyone's looking anymore. I put up some more flyers last weekend, but no one's called."

Rosie fished an inhaler out of her purse and puffed, holding the vapor in her lungs. After exhaling, she started another cigarette.

"I can't believe you," Summer said.

"I refuse to let asthma alter my life one bit. Almost everyone I grew up with has an inhaler. The air pollution in the *barrio* or some other bullshit environmental factor." Rosie swilled the rest of her martini. "I'm more worried about our drinking."

"You ever think about chucking the whole thing? You know, quitting?"

"Every fucking day; but then I ask myself, How many people can say the government pays them to fuck with it? The corporate world isn't for me. Uptight Ivy grads would only assume I was an affirmative action case. Besides, I like life closer to the ground. You?"

"Lately, all I seem to think about is opting out. Running away to somewhere far away from here."

"The judges, D.A.s, politicians, they all want you to feel

that way. Attrition is their best friend. You quit, you'd just be giving in to them. Besides, running won't solve anything. You still have to face your problems in the mirror."

Summer wasn't convinced. Sonia had run away. Maybe she wasn't dead. Maybe she had found happiness. Maybe Summer could, too.

Rosie flicked ashes on her plate. "Promise you'll call me before quitting. Give me a chance to talk you out of it."

Summer didn't tell Rosie she had already phoned Eddie Brockton, but he was out of town for a couple of days. Summer hadn't left a message. "It's a deal."

"What do you think of Gundy getting it?"

Summer swirled her martini, then sipped. "Are any of us sorry he's dead?"

"Who do you think did it?" Rosie asked. "I'm still banking on Marsalis."

"If it was, they'll never get him. He'll concoct an airtight alibi, use phone records to prove he was at home at the time of the murder."

"Are you saying he can alter phone company records?"

Summer held her empty glass up to the light and smiled.

"Shit." Rosie took another drag. "You know what I hated most about Gundy? He was always staring at my tits and ass. I used to dread riding the elevator alone with him. The last time I saw him, he'd just resigned from Sex Crimes and signed on to the Gang Task Force. He told me the first thing he was going to do was investigate my relationship with The Latin Brothers. I told him the only contact I had with the old gang was as their court-appointed attorney. Know what he did?"

Summer waited.

"Pinched my ass."

Touched by Rosie's confidence, Summer said, "Gundy hit on me from day one. Wouldn't take no for an answer. I finally told him if he didn't cease and desist I'd file charges."

Rosie's eyes grew. The secrets women kept from one another. "I never knew *you* were going through it, too! What happened after that?"

"He turned off the little charm he had and made my life hell. I'm sure he sent me sex pics in the mail, the heads of the women cut out."

"Seriously? I heard he was going to make a run for the Senate. Thank God the wicked hick *está muerte*."

Summer picked up the glasses and weaved into the kitchen. Through a window she could see lights skimming off the ocean, a ship pulling away from shore, and wondered where it was heading. She lived alone, surrounded by wood and windows. No boyfriend. No cat, no dog. No plants. Because nothing survived for long in her world. She suddenly felt the prick of her isolation and wondered if she wasn't, like Sonia, trying to make herself disappear.

She shook two more martinis: gin, straight up, very cold, very dry, pickled tomatoes instead of olives, and overflowed both glasses. Summer tried to calculate how much gin she would have to drink before the depression would lift. A quarter of a bottle left: not enough.

She balanced the glasses on a plate and carried them to the living room. Rosie was scanning Summer's bookcase. Summer thought about telling her: *Soon you'll have to carry on without me.*

The telephone buzzed and Summer steadied herself. "Hi."
"It's Jon."
Summer was careful not to slur. "Just the man I wanted to

talk to." She paused, searching for the best way to tell him. But not in front of Rosie.

Levi's voice crackled over the phone line. "Turn on Channel Six."

Summer fumbled for the remote and zapped the set. Policemen were chasing a woman, running wildly, who then slipped through a fence. The picture was grainy.

Summer tried to sober up enough to digest what was happening.

"What's this?" Rosie asked, crouching in front of the TV.

Summer turned up the sound. A local news anchor was saying, "…police were searching the home and dojo of feminist martial artist Stephanie Killington, known by the initials SK, when she bolted. This was captured on video by a bystander with a cell phone. Police caught up to SK at the old Willoughby Warehouse, where a party was in progress."

Summer moved closer to the set, watching as the scene shifted to the building's interior. A crush of twenty-somethings, their minds swelled by ecstasy and cocaine, were dancing and making out in various states of dress and undress. A rave. When SK tore through—the police hurtling after—pandemonium ensued.

"A-fuckin'-mazin'," Levi said, bringing Summer back to the phone. "I go out to dinner and a movie with the wife and kids, come home, turn on the tube, and this is what I see. They've been replaying it as an exclusive."

"When did this happen?" Summer asked.

"About six hours ago."

"Give yourself up, girl," Rosie called to the TV. "You're just making it worse."

Levi said, "Is that Rosie?"

"Yes." Summer whispered, "Oh my god. Motive."

"The strongest motive," Levi said. "Revenge."

The TV flickered. SK was cornered. A dozen cops, wary of her martial arts skills, trained their weapons on her, but didn't move in until she was face-down. They cuffed her and led her away. Then a commercial break. Rosie used the remote to sift for more news.

"I've been told she's going to need a free attorney, so I'm putting you on your first murder case," Levi said. "Reward for winning that video-rape case."

Summer felt a chill. "SK? I... I can't do it."

Rosie put down the remote. "Who's on the phone?"

"Jon."

"You've been bugging me for a murder case for months," Levi said. "Now you're going to bail on me?"

"I've decided... been thinking." This wasn't going like she'd imagined it would.

Rosie crowded her. "SK? He wants you to defend SK?"

"It's funny," Levi said. "You used to pester me for felony cases, wanting to advance your career. Then you were like, 'No more felony cases, Jon, I got too many as is, but when you're ready to give me a murder case, dot dot dot.' So here I am offering you the juiciest murder case we've had in years, and you're turning it down? The local press is all over this. She's a feminist, a lot of Haze County folk detest her, and I need the best P.D. I've got on the case. And facts being facts, it's important that it be a woman. Take the case. You owe me."

"He wants you to defend SK?" Rosie tugged at Summer's elbow.

Summer nodded until she was dizzy.

"Holy shit," Rosie said.

Being around Gundy in the afterworld was more than Summer had bargained for. "I know I owe you—"

"The arraignment's tomorrow," Levi interrupted.

Summer trapped the phone between her neck and shoulder.

"Court Nine, one o'clock," Levi added. "Be prepared for a media circus."

Summer sighed. "OK, OK."

She could hear Levi yawn. "That's a load off my mind. Meet me—"

"Tomorrow, nine, one, circus, I'll be there."

Summer hung up.

———•◦•———

Summer had left Rosie passed out on her couch and was outside, gulping night air and trying to clear her head. She was walking along the beach in front of her home, the sand cold and itchy on her feet, wearing shorts and an oversized t-shirt. She looked to the horizon, a charcoal canvas striated with clouds. Her mouth was puffy and dry. Summer could feel the edge of a headache. She cursed Rosie and whoever invented gin.

She walked to the surf's lip and let the water wash over her feet. She moved forward, toward the clouds speeding across the horizon, toward the light in the distance, the ship.

SK, she thought. She was going to be defending SK. Even before having met her, Summer was reeling under the pressure. She didn't know if she was up to the challenge. She should have stood up to Jon, turned him down. She didn't know if she could cope with all this.

A wave kicked at her knees. She continued treading toward that ship's light. She thought about booking passage, taking it to wherever it was going, to places covered in rainforest flora and fauna, to dark continents and mysterious cultures, to any place she could feel safe, as far away from here as possible.

The water lapped at her chest. Her t-shirt was heavy on her shoulders.

Summer was overwhelmed by sadness. Not just because her whole life had been turned upside down by Gundy. She was alone. Wib, her father, had died of a heart attack four years before, weeks after Summer graduated from law school—the last time she ever saw her parents together. He and Sonia had separated a couple of years before that, Wib moving to a desert condo while Sonia kept the house. Sonia was the one who'd found Wib's body, two days a corpse. He had died alone.

After that, Sonia began a descent into madness. She refused to go outside or let anyone in. After a lifetime of primping and pandering to her looks, she stopped taking care of herself. All of a sudden, Summer found herself in the role of parent, the child taking care of the adult.

She could hear her mother's plaintive wails. It was my fault. I should have never left him. If I had been there, I could have called the paramedics.

Shhh, Summer would say. *The doctor says there was nothing you could have done, even if you had been there.*

I abandoned him. I'm to blame.

After years of wishing that her mother would accept responsibility for something, anything, Summer had found herself trying to convince her that she wasn't responsible.

Eight months ago, when Sonia found out she had incurable melanoma, Summer noticed that a calmness had settled over her mother. She disappeared days later. Summer hadn't seen or heard from her since.

Summer looked out at the ship one last time, then dove deep under the water until her ears popped.

When she felt her lungs were about to burst, she bobbed up to the surface, greedily sucking in air, choosing life.

She swam to shore.

After changing into a dry tank top and gym shorts, Summer lay on the floor, gazing at her ceiling. Three a.m. had slipped into four. Rosie was still curled up on her couch, snoring softly.

Summer was startled by the phone. Rosie shifted but didn't wake.

She picked up. "Jon?"

"No."

"Who is this?"

"Your favorite client."

Summer shut her eyes. She wished that when she opened them, this wouldn't be happening. "I'm not your attorney anymore."

"Nevertheless, congratulations. You escaped the conspiracy. This time."

Marsalis had tracked down her unlisted number. Hanging up would accomplish nothing; she had to play this out. "What conspiracy?"

"Raines charging you with aiding and abetting."

"How did you—" she cut herself off. "So you read the papers."

"Did Bragg include 'Vee have vays ov making you talk' in his article?"

Summer swallowed hard.

Marsalis continued. "Cruz will get his sweetheart deal, as promised. But the D.A. will swear Levi to secrecy, keep it out of the press. And Levi will agree."

His predictions were the product of craft, logic, and surveillance. Summer figured Marsalis had gained access to the hearing's transcript by cracking the courthouse computer network. As for the rest, that was just a matter of connecting the dots. In fact, Summer had arrived at much the same conclusions.

But she decided to test the waters. "How do you know?"

"Like I know everything. Like I know all about Sonia—where she is and what she did. Like I know everything about you, things you don't even know."

Summer's heart pounded. "Where is my mother?"

"First, this important information from our sponsor. Turn on your television. You won't be sorry."

Summer knew she would be but picked up the remote anyway. "What channel?"

Marsalis chuckled softly. "It doesn't matter."

Summer clicked on the set and Rosie appeared. She was in deep sleep but in real time, her hand cupped under her breast, her thumb in her mouth. The picture peeled away to reveal Summer, clenching the remote. The camera zoomed in and her face haunted the whole screen.

She placed the phone back in its cradle and stared at herself staring at herself.

CHAPTER 6

A S FAR AS SUMMER WAS CONCERNED, arraignment court
was one big fat Freudian id. Angiers's courtroom was
chock-a-block with the usual post-weekend crime crush, the
air stale and used up, recycled though hundreds of lungs.
Mothers, girlfriends, and brothers (rarely fathers in this age of
single-parent households) cried over the perps detained in the
cage. Crime-chasing lawyers, their ties loose around their
necks, swept the room and the hallway outside, looking for
anybody with a grand salted away.

While Angiers heard a case at one end of the courtroom,
Summer stood at the other, her back grilled against the arraignment cage, facing the local news media—cameramen,
photographers, TV and print reporters—all angling for a shot
of SK, who, along with five dozen other prisoners, was cuffed
inside.

There was a continuous clamor from inside the cage, ob-
scenities directed at the bailiffs and at SK, the lone woman,

who kept her eyes shut, either in silent prayer, Summer thought, or trying to maintain composure.

A Channel Six camerawoman juked left then right, but Summer blocked her shot. The woman didn't dare step out of the press box. Angiers had already warned the swarm: no questions, no missteps, or they would all be booted.

Where the hell was Levi? Summer needed another body. She saw Rosie, racing from client to client, most of whom she had never met—they were merely names at this point, files, allegations—and caught her eye. But Rosie ignored her. Summer gave a mental shrug.

"Looking good, Summer," Eddie Brockton, one of the lawyers shagging clients, called over to her. "You always did have more bounce to the ounce."

Summer imagined throwing up in her mouth. There went her fantasy of moving to a private law firm. She couldn't believe she had been so desperate to escape her life that she'd considered working for him.

Brockton was a one-time D.A. poster boy who'd been axed when cocaine assumed more importance in his life than his career. One night, after Summer had just started work as a public defender and Brockton still worked for the D.A., Summer went out with him and downed too many margaritas, an escapade she since regretted. Not sex, since that hadn't happened. Just the drunken closeness and the sober avoidance that followed.

Brockton swaggered closer. "Free tonight?"

Summer yawned. "Sure, Brockton, after I visit my shrink, refill my Prozac prescription, and slit my wrists."

Brockton laughed. "Ooh. Bitchy women make me hard." He peered through the bars at SK. "But don't you think you should save it for the prosecution?"

Summer pretended to ignore him until she spotted Levi pushing through the unruly media. Brockton said, "Later," winked, and wandered off.

"Where were you?" Summer asked.

"Sorry. I overslept," Levi whispered, cramming his shoulder against hers. "My daughter was up all night with the flu. Didn't you get my text?"

Summer lied. "I forgot my phone," she said. Actually she had left it home to prevent Marsalis from tracking her. "I'm just glad you're here. I didn't know how much longer I could keep the hounds at bay."

"Do you mean that guy you were talking to—or the press?" came a tart drawl from behind.

Summer turned to see SK eyeballing her. She was wearing a tank top that displayed freckled, muscular arms. Her hair, rust-colored and dirty, hung to her nape. "Let them take their video. I want everyone to see this."

"I would strongly advise against that," Levi said. "People see this on the six o'clock news, it'll stick in their minds. Could taint a jury pool, plus damage public perception."

"Who the hell are you?" SK asked. "My lawyer?"

"She is," Levi pointed to Summer. "I'm her boss."

"Public defenders?"

"Yup."

"You're fired."

It took Summer a few seconds to realize SK wasn't kidding.

Levi shrugged and, reluctantly, slid to the side. Then, media delirium: popping flashes, the whir of advancing cameras, the press hollering questions.

From across the room there was the urgent thwack of a gavel. Angiers hustled over from the bench. "Bailiffs! Get this horde out of here. Now!"

The bailiffs moved quickly, rounding up the protesting news hawkers and bullying them to the exit.

Angiers stood alone in the press box. "Freedom of the press does not mean you can come in here and disrupt my court. If any of you step inside these doors ever again, I'll hold you in contempt!"

After the last journalist funneled out the door, the judge calmed. "I believe it is time for the Stephanie Killington case."

He took his place on the bench, a bailiff unlatched the cage door, and Summer followed Levi to a section of the visitors' gallery roped off for attorneys. The bailiff led SK by the elbow, maneuvered her to a spot in front of the judge. Raines, whom Summer hadn't seen come in, planted himself a few steps away.

Angiers flipped open SK's file and skimmed the evidence, the police and medical examiner reports. He looked up. "Ms. Killington. Have you hired an attorney?"

SK glowered at Angiers. "No."

"Can you afford a private attorney?"

"All my money is tied up in the Women's Center. I have no savings of my own."

Angiers nodded. "If you are willing to sign an affidavit stating this to be the case, the court will provide you with representation."

"No way, Judge. No public defender."

Summer looked to Levi for answers. He didn't have any.

Angiers massaged his neck. "Let me get this straight. You do not have funds available for a private attorney, yet you refuse a free one?"

"You got it."

"Please tell me you're not thinking of representing yourself."

"I'm not thinking of representing myself."

"Good," Angiers said. "Better to leave it to the professionals. So, what do you plan on doing for a defense?"

"Before I answer that, Judge, I have to inform the court that I'm being held in a cell a cockroach wouldn't call home. There's no sink, the toilet doesn't flush, it smells bad, real bad, Your Honor, and there isn't any light. I haven't even had a shower."

Raines interrupted. "Your accommodations have nothing to do with—"

The judge hammered down his gavel. "Raines! In my court lawyers have fewer rights than fraternity pledges. Don't talk unless I tell you to."

Raines looked sideways. "I apologize to the court."

"I don't think he means it, Your Honor," SK said.

"I don't either," Angiers said, cracking a smile. Summer couldn't remember the last time he had done that. "Anyway, I can sympathize with your plight, Ms. Killington. But I have no powers outside this court. Take it up with your congressman. I can't even get the jails to provide medical care to prisoners with open wounds."

"I'm being treated like I'm guilty when the law states I'm innocent until—"

"Spare me Civics 101," Angiers roared, suddenly out of patience, "and save me the hassle of reading your mind: *Who* is going to represent you?"

SK shook her chains. "No, Your Honor. This is wrong. I refuse to participate until—"

Angiers slapped the bench with his palms. "Participate?"

"Yes. Participate. Until I'm moved to a decent—"

"Where you are incarcerated while awaiting trial is not my problem. Look behind you, to those gentlemen waiting politely for us to conclude our business so that they may find out if they will have to stand trial. *That* is my problem."

"I'm innocent."

"Claiming you are innocent is irrelevant, Ms. Killington." Angiers peered over his eyeglasses at the file. "I have no choice but to find that there is ample evidence to charge you with the murder of Harold Gundy. Now, for the record, who will be your attorney?"

At the mention of Gundy's name, Summer noticed that the prisoners in the cage quieted, watching SK. But when Summer tried to catch SK's eye, she looked away. *Fine*, Summer thought, *I don't even want this damn case.*

Angiers said, "This is no time to mess around. If you cannot afford a private attorney, then I am forced to appoint a public defender. If you are dissatisfied with your representation, the law allows you certain options, which will be explained to you." He looked over to Levi, who was sitting elbows on knees. "Mr. Levi, will you, at least for the time being, be in charge of Ms. Killington's defense?"

Levi stood. "No, Your Honor, I am here merely to assist. Ms. Neuwirth will have the honors."

Angiers eyed Summer coldly. He had taken a lot of heat over Cruz's missing file and subsequent release. "As you wish. Because of the violent nature of the crime and the accused's martial arts skills, which are documented in this file, I am forced to deny bail."

Summer banged the back of her knee into her chair when she stood. She talked fast: "Your Honor. Ms. Killington has been a model citizen and done much good for the people of Haze County. She's not a likely candidate to flee. At the very least, she should have the right to remain free until a jury decides her fate."

Angiers stared, dumbstruck, then passed his hand across his forehead. "Ms. Neuwirth, when God gave out nerve, you somehow managed to wrangle a subscription. The last client of yours to grace this court lasted one day on his own recognizance before ending up back here on drug charges." He pointed to his photo gallery, where Jimi Cruz's picture was covered by a yellow stickie. "If I let Ms. Killington free on bail, no doubt you'll have her on a plane to Tijuana in time for the next bullfight. Speaking of bull, request denied. Next case."

Before Summer could respond, Levi gave her a keep-cool tap on the shoulder.

But SK wasn't finished. "Your Honor. I'm innocent."

"I *said*, next case," Angiers said.

"Don't send me back to that hellhole."

Angiers said simply, "Bailiff. Remove the prisoner."

When the bailiff nudged her, SK turned his momentum against him, and in one easy motion, tripped him to the floor. She stood her ground, hands still shackled. "I didn't murder anyone! This is all a mistake!" When the bailiff jumped up to grab her, she pushed him down again with her foot.

Bedlam erupted. While the perps in the cage woofed and spectators crowded for a better view, the other bailiffs descended on her. SK didn't resist. She let them corral her from behind, lift her off the ground, until the one she had tripped, his face balled up in anger, rushed over, club drawn.

"No!" Summer leaped forward to intervene, but Levi held her back.

For a split second, Summer saw a smile crease SK's face. Then, suspended a foot off the ground by the struggling bailiffs, she doubled him over with a kick so laser-quick that Summer almost blinked through it.

The other bailiffs shackled her feet and carted her off, while the prisoners jangled their chains. It started as a low clanking that picked up when they added foot stomps, whistles, and then a chant: *Fuck the system.*

Angiers tried to bring the court to order, but others in the visitors' gallery joined in, until the entire courtroom rumbled.

The chanting and chain music continued long after SK was gone.

CHAPTER 7

S UMMER WISHED THE HANDS PROBING HER BREASTS weren't so cold, so flinty. She closed her eyes, waiting it out. Goosebumps rode up her neck, under the sweat.

She was twisted around, face-to-wall. She didn't resist. Fluorescent light buzzed above, blinding her, the wall painted institutional gray. Fingers ran down her leg, then up the other. Summer took it.

The butch prison guard leered at Summer. "Proceed," she grunted.

Summer hated visiting clients at the jail, hated the barbed wire lining the roof and the armed guards paroling there, hated being frisked, hated being drawn into her clients' pathetic lives and lies. She promised herself that if she ever ended up here as an inmate, she would kill herself. Never would she be able to cede control of her life to a fixed schedule: a gray breakfast at 7, mindless work detail from 8 to 4, exercise for an hour, TV, lights out at 10. The mindless death scared her as much as prison violence.

Summer tucked her blouse into her skirt and stepped through the metal detector. She was buzzed through another door, into another guard station.

"I'll take over, Maggie," Joseph Spivak, another guard, called over the intercom. "Why, Summer and me, we go way back. Her dad and I were like this—" he held his fist up to the portal.

Maggie pushed back her cap and nodded, like she had heard it all before, and returned to her post.

Summer pecked Spivak on the cheek. When Wib died, Spivak had taken care of the funeral arrangements and comforted Sonia. Summer was so grateful, she'd let him take over the mortgage on Wib's condo, where he guzzled beer, watched sports, grew tomatoes, and raised Dobermans.

"Hey, Spiv," she said, "what are you doing here?"

"Saw from the visitors log you were on your way in; figured I should be your tour guide."

Summer scrunched up her nose, not at the prospect of Spiv acting as her escort—which was, she admitted, a relief—but at the flat odor that permeated the air, a cloying mixture of unwashed inmates, institutional chow, bug poison, and detergent.

"Before we head in," she said, "could I have my notebook and a pen back? I'm having a meeting with a client, not digging her out of here with a ballpoint."

Spiv yawned. His belly strained against his uniform, tufts of white undershirt briefly visible, reminding Summer of a plastic pack of tissues. "Orders is orders, Sunshine. In the hands of some of these fruitcakes, pens can be weapons. When I worked the men's side, I once saw a guy carve out his own Adam's apple. Blood everywhere. Lots of crazy shit down here."

Summer had a formula for calculating the veracity of Spiv's tales: subtract two-thirds. If he said it took fifteen guards to bust up a riot, it was five. If he claimed he earned a few hundred by selling his urine to another guard trying to beat a drug test, the thought had probably just crossed Spiv's mind, and that thought became the story.

"First time in maximum security?" Spiv asked, as they headed down a sterile corridor.

"Yeah."

"You're in for a treat."

They took the corrugated steel elevator to the bottom, where they were buzzed through two more doors, and then proceeded down a flight of brick steps.

Spiv blew his nose and sighed. "What would your father think about you defending a D.A. killer?"

"Aren't there some steps missing?" Summer asked. "Like a trial and a verdict?"

"What would your father think about you defending an *alleged* D.A. killer?"

"That's better. Probably"—she imitated Wib's croak—"'Where'd I go wrong raisin' you? Workin' for crooks, scum, and pervs. I musta fucked up if I didn't teach you respect for the law.'"

Spiv laughed. "Hey, that's pretty good. Wib never liked Gundy. Hell, from what I've heard, nobody did. I don't know how he could walk with that skyscraper up his ass. But at least he took out the trash."

Wib, Summer knew, had felt much the same way. His qualms with Gundy had centered on Gundy's penchant for playing to public opinion. Drug sweeps, sex solicitation roundups, drunk driver roadblocks, fag spa shutdowns, misdemeanor offenses that strained the court system and forced cops off the streets to deal with the paperwork.

Spiv waved to a ceiling-mounted camera, and they were buzzed through another door into a stretch of hallway. The farther they walked, the worse the stench—feces, urine, and other signs of human decay. But it was the sounds, the eerie wails of insanity, that put Summer on edge.

There were a dozen cells set in cement, with two-inch-thick doors, each with a tiny window. As Summer passed, women pounded on the portals, their bulging eyes distorted by the glass. Caged bulbs lining the hall provided ghostly light.

Summer held her nose. "Who are you, the Marquis de Spivak? Maximum security is for convicted psychos, not for people awaiting trial. Move my client to a decent cell."

Spiv grinned. "She'd be having more fundy if she hadn'ta whacked Gundy." When Summer scowled, he added sternly, "Don't give me a hard time. You got a problem, take it up with the warden."

"Maybe I will," Summer said. "At the least, I want to talk with my client in private, inside."

Spiv buzzed his lips. "That's a negative. If I were you, after what she pulled in Angiers's court today, I wouldn't be so anxious to spend time alone with her. It took, like, ten guys to carry her out."

Summer poked his shoulder three times. "Three. I was there, remember? Maybe the bailiffs should have asked her nicely."

Spiv stepped aside and peered through the window. He motioned Summer over with fluttering fingers and hissed, "Look at this."

Summer stood on tiptoes and pushed her face against the scratchy glass. SK was inside, her Haze County Jail jumpsuit unzipped to her navel, the sleeves rolled up to her shoulders. She was sparring with her shadow. Her hair flew with each kick and punch. Sweat sparkled on her forehead.

Spiv whispered into Summer's ear. "She could kill you before you could even yelp."

This time Spiv wasn't exaggerating. In fact, the thought had crossed Summer's mind earlier, the moment SK sent Angiers's bailiff crumbling. She ran a hand over her glassy stomach. "I'm going in. Alone."

"She could crack your neck, smash your nose through your brain. Lots of ways to kill someone with just your fists. I've seen it."

"Beat it, Spiv."

"Nah-ah-ah," he said, staccato-like. "I'll be right here. Watching."

"Any excuse to ogle pretty girls."

Spiv chuckled as he tapped the glass with his stun gun and unlatched the window. He called inside, "Stay away from the door."

SK kept fighting her shadow.

"Ten minutes," he told Summer. "That's it."

After Spiv bolted the door behind her, Summer flashed a business card. "Remember me, your court-appointed attorney?"

Punch-punch-kick-punch. Summer could hear SK's hands and feet snap air.

Summer put the card back in her pocket. "They didn't rough you up too much when they brought you back from arraignment, did they?"

SK continued to pretend she wasn't there. Summer took a moment to look around. The toilet was molded steel, the pipes leaking, and the flush handle broken off. There was no sink.

The mattress was chewed up, the foam padding ripped out and scattered. Pointing at the mattress, she said, "You didn't do that, did you?"

SK talked while she sparred. "It was like that when I got here."

"They're not known for their maid service here."

SK grunted.

There was never an easy way to start. "I'd like to ask you about what happened. From the beginning."

SK responded by ducking imagined blows.

"I'm trying to help," Summer said.

SK concentrated on her training. Summer was almost relieved. If SK refused to talk with her, she might be able to convince Levi to assign someone else, maybe Rosie, who would be happy to match her fire with SK's ire. Summer tried one last time—sans diplomacy. "What's your fucking problem?"

Finally a question SK deemed worthy of a response. She finished her workout with a flourish of kicks and slumped on the bench. After taking a few seconds to catch her breath, she spoke without looking at Summer. "A public defender kept the man who murdered my husband out of jail. Now he's free and I'm here in this sewer suite. Alone. No husband. No family. Just me."

"You blame me because another P.D. got a client you don't like an acquittal with an insanity defense?"

"Yes."

"Funny. Most of my clients don't begin blaming me until after the verdict is in."

SK scowled. She zipped up her jumpsuit and backhanded sweat beads from her forehead. "How long have you been a public defender?"

"Four years."

"What's your success rate?"

"You mean, how many acquittals have I gotten?"

"Yeah."

Summer watched a bug scurry across the floor. SK was wrong. Lots of cockroaches called this cell home. "I don't get to cherry pick."

"How many?"

"One."

SK shut her eyes and shook her head. "How many murder trials?"

Summer hesitated. "This is my first."

SK buried her face in her hands and spoke through her fingers. "You want me to be a guinea pig for some Barbie doll bureaucrat who's won exactly once and never worked a murder case in her life?"

Summer's forehead felt hot; her heart beat so hard that her vision blurred. She glanced through the portal at Spiv. He caught her eye and splayed his fingers over the glass. Five minutes. "If you're that unsatisfied, you can file what's called a Marsden. Usually the court is reluctant to approve a change merely because of a personality conflict, but give it a try. Perhaps we can find you another public defender more to your liking. But until you retain another lawyer, I'm it."

SK's expression betrayed nothing.

Summer kept pressing. "If you're as innocent as you claim, let's get to work so we can get you out of here."

She followed SK's eyes as they took in the cell. Summer had seen this look before in clients: *Am I going to spend the rest of my life here?*

She seized the moment. "Where were you the night Gundy died?"

SK relented. "In bed. With a cold."

Summer didn't give her time to stonewall. Keep the questions coming. Don't let her hedge. "Did anyone see you there?"

"No."

"Did you make or receive any telephone calls that night?"

"No."

"No one can confirm where you were at that time?"

SK shook her head.

"Did you seek medical attention, or can anyone verify you were ill?"

"It was just a bug, a 24-hour kind of thing."

"Blood matching Gundy's was found on a glass fragment embedded in one of your boots. How do you think it got there?"

SK raised an eyebrow. It was the first time she had displayed interest in anything Summer said. "What boots?"

"A pair of black St. Croix brand leather boots, size 7 1/2."

SK crossed her arms, clenched her elbows with her hands, and hunched her shoulders, as if this would help her figure things out. If she was acting, Summer had to admit she was very good. It took a few seconds before SK managed to say, "I haven't worn those boots in weeks, months maybe."

Summer bit her lip. The first lie was key, a foundation for the rest. But whose lie? SK's? The police's? No matter what, Summer would have to construct SK's case around it. But she didn't have time now to explore now. "After Gundy let Brauer cop an insanity plea, you threatened to kill him the day Brauer walked."

SK got up to pace. Summer could see she was struggling against tears. "My late husband and I were very close. He was the reason I turned my life around. But after the funeral, I realized killing Gundy wouldn't accomplish anything. I could do more by carrying on my husband's work."

Spiv knocked on the glass and playfully gave Summer the finger.

"Time's up," Summer said. "I'll be back."

"Wait!" SK rushed toward her.

Startled, Summer backpedalled.

"Whoa." SK stopped, palms up. "I… I didn't do it."

"I heard you at the arraignment."

SK spat a swirl of denials. She hadn't been at Gundy's that night. She'd been as shocked as anyone when she heard the news. She would never take the law into her own hands. It was all a big mistake. Or she'd been framed. But she was innocent.

All of Summer's clients denied their crimes, even after plea bargaining; denied them to the cops, to their neighbors, to their cell mates, and especially to their lawyer. Deny, deny some more, until they began to believe it themselves.

Summer heard Spiv unbolt the door. "Last question today: How did police photos of your late husband—with your fingerprints—end up in Gundy's apartment?"

SK swallowed hard. "I left them there."

PART II

REASONABLE DOUBTS

CHAPTER 8

SUMMER SQUEEZED INTO HER OFFICE with Levi, sipping coffee. The walls were lead-chip white, bare except for a bulletin board tacked with layers of index cards with scribbled notes and a calendar of Ansel Adams landscapes. Summer, because she liked surprises, rarely flipped ahead.

Levi had his feet up on her desk, the only place there was room for them. "Guess who I had dinner with last night? I'll give you a hint: If you poured water into him, he'd leak."

Summer lifted Levi's feet off her desk, slid over to the coffee maker, refilled her cup, lifted his feet again, and made her way back to her chair. "Jimi Cruz?"

Levi couldn't contain his smile.

"You visited my favorite trustafarian at the jail?" Summer asked.

"Better than that," Levi said. "I got Raines to let him go, provided he leave town."

Just as Marsalis had predicted. Summer's heart shimmied.

"When *I* suggested Cruz clear out, Raines tried to get me disbarred."

"Oh, so now you admit telling him to scram."

Summer regretted that admission. She had to be more careful, had to keep her mind on her work. She bunched her hair up and fanned her neck with her hand. "Good thing I'm covered under lawyer-client confidentiality," she joked.

"Good thing," Levi repeated, obviously annoyed. "Well, timing is everything. I picked Cruz up at the jail, threw him in my car, handed him a couple of burgers and a couple twenties, and drove him to the bus station. I made sure he got on the bus and waved bye-bye." Levi checked his watch. "He ought to be panhandling in Vegas by now."

"Probably already making some Las Vegas P.D.'s life miserable," Summer said. The hearing, Raines's threats, Hightower's letter of complaint to the Bar Association, all that stress, all for nothing. "What did you have to barter for Raines's enlightened generosity?"

"I had to promise to keep it real quiet so the press, especially Bragg, wouldn't get wind."

When Summer sighed, she spilled coffee on her blouse. "O-o-oh," she groaned.

"Good thing you drink it black, so it won't stain," Levi said. "When you get home, boil some water and pour it over your blouse like it's a coffee filter."

Summer dabbed at the stain with a napkin. "Sometimes I'm not sure whether you're more like a mother or more like a father."

"Neither," Levi said.

Summer tossed the damp napkin in the trash. "We know Raines didn't suddenly develop a conscience, so what made him change his mind?"

"He probably figured the negative PR wasn't worth it, especially with you on the SK case."

"He's banking on the fact that SK's case will do more damage to me than any charges he could raise with Cruz." Summer took a long sip. "He's probably right, too."

Levi snatched SK's file off Summer's desk. "Ready?"

Summer tried not to look as Levi pulled Gundy's death pics out of the folder and neatly ordered them on the floor, one by one, angle by angle, Gundy by Gundy, until neither of them could walk without stepping on them.

Rosie walked with sulky steps by the open door, carrying an armful of legal books.

"Hey!" Summer called.

But Rosie didn't stop. Summer heard her sigh loudly and drop the books in her office. She got to the door just as Rosie poked her head in.

"What?" Rosie said.

"You mad at me?" Summer asked, lowering her voice.

"No."

"Then why have you been avoiding me?"

She buzzed her lips. "I haven't been avoiding you. I've just got, you know, work to do."

Rosie's tone stung Summer. She stepped carefully between Gundy's bloody pictures and sat on the edge of her desk. Was she being paranoid? Was their friendship fracturing? She needed Rosie's easy camaraderie now more than ever. "We're talking about SK," she said.

"I can see that," Rosie said, taking in the photos.

"I could really use your help."

"There's no place to sit." When Summer and Levi shot her

vinegary glances, Rosie said, "OK, OK," and dropped to her knees.

They were quiet as they studied what the murderer had done to Harold Gundy. Summer felt a headache coming on; she had an irrational need for a cigarette, as if the nicotine would drive away the dizzies and the thickness clawing her stomach.

Get a grip, she commanded herself. She started with the broken railing, the puzzles of glass spread around the floor, but it got ugly fast—Gundy lying in blood and mescal, shards of the bottle nearby, close-ups of his crushed skull, the eerie marks on his back. The marks. Summer couldn't take her eyes off them: ancient symbols, or designs created in the brain of a madman—or woman.

Levi spoke first. "We can assume, judging by the nature of his injuries, that Gundy was thrown from his second floor loft onto a glass coffee table. But the ME claims the fall didn't kill him, although he suffered internal injuries consistent with a hard fall. It was the blow to the head."

"Like I always say, mescal is some nasty shit," Rosie said. She picked up a photo. "Why are Gundy's pants pulled down around his ankles?"

"You think he could have been doing the deed alone, got startled, and accidently busted through the wooden railing?" Levi asked.

"Oh, that's a compelling defense," Rosie said, smacking her forehead.

Levi shrugged. "What's the ME report say?"

"Nega—" Summer hacked at a ball of phlegm in her throat. "Negative on any semen. If Gundy was seeking sexual gratification, he came up short."

"Prolly wouldn't have been the first time," Levis said. "Any possibility the pants came down after he was killed?"

"Not according to the M.E.," Summer said.

Rosie picked up another photo and held it close. "His skull was caved in. Can we assume these are bottle fragments mixed in with the shards of the table?"

Summer was barely listening, her attention focused on a detail within the crime photo: pictures of Jonathan Sadbury, SK's late husband. The word "shame" was scrawled on them.

"It's pretty grim." Her voice cracked, so she cleared her throat. "Strong motive, no alibi, his, uh, blood found in SK's home, her fingerprints on his front door *and* on the pictures Gundy was clutching when the police found him."

Levi blew on his coffee. "You know Raines will portray that as Gundy identifying his murderer before croaking. A deathbed clue always plays well with a jury."

"What we need is an eye witness." Summer skimmed the file. "No witnesses yet, but the D.A. doesn't have to give me any of that until a judge is assigned."

"Even then they'll probably dick you around," Rosie said. "You know how they like to play the delay game."

"Not this time," Levi said. "It's high-profile for Haze County, and they figure it's a slam-dunk win for them. My hunch is they'll bend over backwards to give you everything you ask for, so there's no way you can cry foul."

"It's sad that it takes Gundy's murder to elicit cooperation from the D.A.," Summer said. "So you think they're going with a circumstantial case?"

"Perhaps, perhaps not." Levi squinted at a close-up of Gundy's glass-riddled side; then, shuddering, turned it face-down on the carpet. "The cops are going to be extra cautious with the investigation. If they locate a witness, they're going to check out his testimony before clueing you in. But I also think, given the circumstances, that Raines is going to feign graciousness."

Summer asked, "Do you think he'll extend this graciousness by using his influence to get SK moved to a decent cell? She's being held in Dante-like conditions. It'd sure help me wrangle more cooperation out of her."

"How'd your meeting go?" Levi asked.

"I got her to talk a little bit, but she's not exactly thrilled with me. She might even do a Marsden."

"If that happens, I'll take her," Rosie said.

"If she's successful, you can have her," Summer said.

Levi mulled. "Let me work on getting her moved. I've piled up a few chits with the warden over the years. Assuming this goes to trial, I want you to paper Judge Kelly if he's assigned. You know how tight he and the court magistrate are."

"We're still pushing him off cases?" Summer asked.

Rosie twirled hair around her finger. "I had him a couple of weeks ago, when we thawed. The only good thing is my client will probably get another trial on appeal, since Kelly totally fucked him."

"He hasn't done a trial in weeks," Levi said, "so he'll express interest in any case. I hear the other judges are mighty pissed with him. Hope this teaches him lesson, though I'm not counting on it."

"What's with the lipstick marks on the back?" Rosie asked.

"It's maroon," Levi teased. "Your shade."

"Every shade is Rosie's shade," Summer said. A memory fragment: Wib putting down the telephone, pulling down the shades, the only time she could remember him scared. Summer was eleven, twelve maybe. Wib being stalked, the family threatened, another time, another place, but the same marks.

"Jon," Summer said, "were you around for the Sean Strickland case?"

Levi belched silently. "Not that it ever got to us, but yeah, I remember. About, what, more than a dozen years ago? A serial freak who had it in for law enforcement—a cop, D.A., his parole officer. Left some weird calling card."

"Strickland bashed his victims' skulls in, then drew marks on their backs after they were dead. My father was the cop on that case." What she didn't tell him was that he had almost been a victim, too.

"If Strickland weren't already maggot food, he'd certainly be a suspect."

"They never positively identified his body because he blew up with his car. What if Strickland isn't dead? What if he's back?"

Rosie laughed. "Why would *he* frame SK? Don't forget the physical evidence. It's pretty damning."

Levi idly fanned himself with one of the pictures. "Are you going to conduct an investigation? Because if you start poking around, looking for Strickland, then Raines will turn it around on you, claim SK mutilated Gundy's body to divert suspicion from her. Plus, an investigation takes manpower; which, as you know, is in short supply around here. I would strongly advise you not to lift up this rock and see what's crawling underneath. Your first murder case is no time to get fancy."

Summer dumped her coffee dregs. "If I don't, then we both know SK doesn't stand a chance."

Rosie stood up and readjusted her skirt. "Listen to Jon. He's old, been around the block a few kajillion times."

"Thanks," Levi said.

"There's more than enough work for you without you pretending to be some private dick," Rosie continued.

"Then I'd better get started," Summer said.

Rosie stood. "I can see I was a lot of help here. Summer, you are making one *muy grande* mistake if you start an investigation."

Summer turned off the coffee maker. "I'm trying to save this woman's life."

"Whatever you say." Rosie left. Summer could heard her through the sheetrock walls, rustling around her office.

"What's gotten into her?" Levi asked.

"I don't know." Summer really didn't.

Levi shrugged. "Hormones."

"I heard that," Rosie shouted through the wall.

Summer laughed, the only light moment of the day. "Who's the private detective on the case?" She picked up the photos and jammed them back into the file.

Levi talked into his cup. "New guy. His name's Tai Sanborn."

Rosie came flying out of her office as if she didn't own footsteps. She filled Summer's doorway again, breathing hard. "A cop?"

"*Ex*-cop," Levi said. "On disability."

Summer flipped the file on her desk. "You're trying him out on a murder case?"

"I'm trying *you* out on a murder case," Levi retorted, "and nobody's complained."

"What happened to Rothstein, Jon?"

"On maternity leave."

"How about Sam Nell?"

"He quit. Got tired of too many hours for too little pay."

"But why Tai Sanborn?"

"He's the only P.I. around not pulling thirty-five cases," Levi said. "He's ex-homicide. Could be helpful."

"And?"

"I had no choice. The 1990 Americans With Disabilities Act mandates we hire him. If I don't assign him a case now, Raines promised me federal prosecutors would come a-calling."

Summer chucked the coffee filter into the trash. "He's probably a D.A. plant. Even if he isn't, you know how fat and lazy ex-cops are. They leak information to their buddies on the force and don't do what they're told. I never met an ex-cop who even knew the expression 'innocent until proven guilty.' And the last thing I need on this case is some guy faking a back injury so—"

A man in patched, faded jeans, paisley shirt hanging out, had come up behind Rosie. He had crescent-shaped eyes, and dimples highlighted his smirk. He was too good-looking, too at ease, to have business here.

"I'm looking for Summer Neuwirth," he said.

"You found her. And you are?"

He grinned. "Tai Sanborn. The fat, lazy ex-cop with the fake back injury."

CHAPTER 9

RAINES WAITED FOR SUMMER OUTSIDE the calendar magistrate's office. His suit was wrinkly—she was sure he had slept in it—and so was he. The undersides of his eyes were cupped by bruise-colored circles. The trial hadn't started and already both of them were stressing.

Raines spoke in hushed tones. "I have to inform you of a recent development in the Gundy case."

"Sidney," Summer said louder than usual, "you sound positively defensive."

"Shhh." Raines looked around in spy movie fashion. "I just want to make it clear that my office is prosecuting this case by the book. The police discovered some sophisticated surveillance equipment in Harold's condo. Someone wired up the place real good, someone who knows his stuff, too, judging by the look of it. I'll have the details messengered to your office."

Summer's heart hopscotched a beat. Now she was whispering. "Are you saying there may be video of Gundy's murder?"

"All I know is the house was wired for sound and video, attached to a laptop computer concealed in the floor boards of the loft. We figure it was connected to a remote server, but there's no way to find out where it's located or who put it there. The police must have tripped an alarm because access was cut. No fingerprints on the equipment, no audio or video stored on the premises, no clues—"

"You have no idea who put it there?"

"I've checked with our department and the police."

"And?"

"It's not ours."

"Could it be FBI, CIA, DEA?"

"Don't know."

"I assume you have the cops chasing down every electronics dealer in town."

"You know I can't comment on an investigation in progress."

Summer coughed to stop herself from slapping the smirk off his face. "Beautiful, Sidney."

"We're as anxious to find out who did this as you are," Raines retorted.

"Until you do, drop the charges against SK."

"Dream on, Summer. It'll bolster our case, no matter who put it there."

Summer wagged a finger. "Only if it's admissible. Which it won't be unless you can show where it came from."

Raines held the door open for Summer. "If we get access to video that shows SK murdered Gundy, no judge in the county would exclude it."

Summer knew he was right. She stepped into the calendar magistrate's office.

"But no matter what," Raines continued, "we're going murder one, death penalty all the way. We'll throw in murder two and manslaughter just to round it out. But I guarantee your client's going to fry."

"I thought you ghouls relied on lethal injection these days," Summer said. "Less messy."

Raines rippled his slight shoulders. "I will grant you one favor, though. We'll skip the resisting arrest and assault charges." Actually, Raines was only doing himself a favor, since no prosecutor liked to muddle a murder case—and confuse a jury—with a series of lesser charges.

"Assault?"

"The bailiff."

"Oh, right," Summer said. "But of course you'd be opening the prosecution up to a charge of brutality."

Raines popped a cough drop into his mouth and smiled.

The calendar magistrate checked a chart behind him and settled on Judge Wesley Kelly, whose docket was empty. Summer and Raines climbed the stairs to his courtroom, where she dropped off the paper work to exclude him with the clerk. All the way there and back, Raines pretended she didn't exist, didn't say another word to her.

The magistrate didn't seem surprised when they returned. He consulted the chart, then assigned SK's case to the next available judge: Morton Hightower.

Raines crunched the last bit of cough drop. "You should have seen this coming, Summer. You sure you're ready for a murder trial?"

CHAPTER 10

SUMMER WAS HAVING TROUBLE FOCUSING on her work, Rosie's distant behavior gnawing at her. Office life had never before been like this. From the moment they had met, Summer and Rosie had had a special chemistry. Levi had hired them at the same time, although this wasn't what forged what Summer had always assumed would be an unshakable bond. It was the older women in the office, graying women in drab pantsuits who had been at the vanguard of the women's movement—the first women public defenders in the state—who had pushed Summer and Rosie together and forced them to rely on each other.

Behind Summer's and Rosie's backs, these women, bitter and territorial, had taunted them, called them the "hair flippers" because of the long hair they constantly swept from their eyes. Levi also became the subject of derision: He was a life-support system for a penis, they chided. He liked hiring pretty girls: office furniture, not hardcore lawyers.

Summer was knocked out of her reverie by Tai, who entered without knocking, poured himself a cup of coffee, and sat down. "I ran down the police witnesses and all the other stuff you requested," he said.

Summer looked up from paperwork. She couldn't even remember what she had been reading. "That was fast. I just got them yesterday, after the judge was assigned."

"That's why you hired me."

"I didn't hire you."

"Right," he said. "I forgot. Who's the judge on the case?"

"Hightower."

Tai whistled. "He can get awful ornery."

"Tell me something I don't know."

"OK. Did you know that Hightower's up for re-election?"

"Of course."

"Did you know he's going to face a primary challenge?"

"Nobody's announced a run against him. He's unbeatable, which is why he's run unopposed three times."

"It's not public yet," Tai responded. "And *you're* the reason Hightower's going to have to earn it this time. Getting that video-rape nut off."

"Who's running against him?"

Tai savored the moment. "Raines."

Summer tried to contain her surprise. "No way."

"He's announcing in a couple days."

"Raines has never expressed political ambitions."

"Whatever." Tai clasped his hands behind his neck, fanned his elbows out and yawned. "Want to know what I found out about Gundy, or talk about why you dislike me so much?"

His yawn was contagious, but Summer stopped herself. "I'd rather hear about Gundy."

Tai held his cup near his mouth while he talked. "I ran down the same witnesses the cops did. The building super wasn't around the night Gundy was offed, but saw SK around Gundy's condo earlier in the day. She's an oldie but a goodie, not too swift, doesn't have great eyesight. She told the cops she could positively ID SK, but she doesn't remember if she was wearing her glasses, so you might be able to impeach her." He sipped, made a *blech* face. "Sugar?"

Summer reached into a drawer and flicked him a couple of packets.

"Milk?" he asked.

Summer pointed to her mini-fridge. Tai leaned over and opened the fridge. He dribbled the last of the milk into his coffee, then ripped open a packet of sugar, stirred, and slurped. "Then there's Malcolm Byers," he continued, "the guy delivering pizza to a neighbor. In the police report, he said he saw a woman with curly red hair run from Gundy's apartment at 10:30 P.M., which fits with the estimated time of death. You've read the report?"

"Yeah."

"Notice how he gives such detail, as though he watched her over and over again?"

"You think the cops led him on?"

He gave Summer a cheeky smile. "If they had, it wouldn't have been so obvious."

"Did he remember what kind of shoes she was wearing?" Summer asked.

"Black boots, same as the cops found."

"That's bad news."

"Perhaps, but Byers is no Boy Scout. Got expelled from high school for stealing. One of his teachers said Byers had attention deficit disorder, although that's with 20-20 hindsight. Back then, they just called it being an asshole. I checked his movie rental record. Lots of ninja flicks and hard-core porn."

Summer eyed Tai warily. "You need a court order for that."

"Can I help it I'm persuasive? Besides, now you know *you'll* need a court order—if you want to use it against him." Tai crossed his legs, sat back lazily. "Not bad for an ex-cop."

"You forgot fat and lazy."

Tai laughed. Nothing seemed to sting him. Summer had to admit he was good, which was almost worse than him being bad, since she didn't trust him. She needed to get him working on something else until she could figure out what he was up to.

"And"—he stuffed the empty sugar packets into the milk carton, stood up, and tossed it behind the back into the trash, and missed—"I tracked down SK's medical records."

Angrily, Summer flung the carton back at him. "What made you think I wanted SK's medical history? The law in this state requires me to turn over evidence harmful to my client to the D.A. You know, Discovery works both ways here."

Tai grimaced, then shot the container into the trash. "Nothing but net," he said. "How the hell am I supposed to turn up anything meaningful if I have to turn over the bad stuff too?"

"The boys who write the laws don't want the defense turning up anything useful," she said. "It could mean big trouble if Raines gets wind."

Tai shrugged. "Want to know what I found out or not?"

Summer stood up and leaned over him, placing her hands on the arm supports of his chair, staring him in the eye. "Stop acting like a cop."

"It's pretty juicy." He was taunting her.

"I mean it."

"SK's medical records show she was pregnant when she was 17."

Summer spun away, rubbing her eyes. "If the D.A. finds out, at the very least they'll leak it to the press and try to influence the jury pool. An abortion to go with priors for prostitution."

"How do you know she had an abortion?" He was so cool, so unflappable. A beach bum with a cop's brain.

"She told me she has no family," Summer said. "Besides, if you were whoring, would you take time off to have a kid?"

"Good point."

"If you don't promise me right now that you will investigate only what I tell you to investigate, I'm dropping you from the case."

Tai eyed the ceiling, then her. "OK, OK. I promise."

"All right. Now I need you to check out something for me."

She told him about Strickland.

Afterward, Tai said, "Quite a stretch. A whole lot of coincidence to digest at once, and tough to prove without a way to ID Strickland's body."

"Back then, they didn't have DNA technology."

"You'd need DNA from Strickland to match against his corpse, assuming they'll let you dig him up."

"I'll take care of that."

Tai stared at Summer.

Summer stared back. "Why are you looking at me like that?"

"I think it's sexy the way you take charge." He downed the last of his coffee. "Not going to report me to the PC police, are you?"

"If I thought it would do any good, I might. Now get out. I have work and so do you. Start collecting background on Strickland."

Tai hoisted himself up. "I'm going, I'm going. First stop, Strickland's hometown. Where was he raised?"

"Birch Creek, but—"

"I know it. About six hundred miles north of here. A real hick town. The town used to have a problem with kids hanging out in the 7-11 parking lot, drinking beer and vandalizing cars. So the store started piping muzak outside. Drove them away."

"Ingenious, but travel's not in the budget," she said. "Jon will never approve it."

"I don't care."

Summer was wary of Tai's eagerness.

Tai seemed to read her thoughts. "Look, it's simple," he said. "To turn up information on someone who's dead, not only *can* you go home again, you have to."

CHAPTER 11

"THIS IS THE BRASS CUP that Winston Taylor, the Vampire of Sedona, used to scoop the blood of victims before drinking it," Gupta Mahakavi, collector of the macabre, told Summer.

Summer had struggled with antiquated microfiche at the library before finding an article dated sixteen years ago describing an auction to raise money for Sean Strickland's victims. Two phone calls and a three-hour drive later, here she was, talking to a retired forensics expert with the world's most extensive collection of serial killer memorabilia.

In an accent spiced with one part Bombay and one part Hollywood action adventure, Mahakavi had eagerly shown Summer display cases crammed with blood-rusted knives, guns, daggers, electric saws, a garbage disposal, garbage bags, ropes, handcuffs, packets of heavy-duty condoms, and other tools of the trade.

"What do the scratches on the side of the cup signify?" Summer asked.

"Winston," Mahakavi said—he called his subjects by their first names—"filed those symbols himself with the same knife used in his crimes. Six marks, six victims."

The cup was still rusted with blood, which made it somehow more palatable than fresh kill, Summer thought. "What drives someone to do things like this?"

"Besides an intense feeling of alienation and grandiosity? It is difficult to generalize. Many of them were abused or abandoned as children, or paranoid, or chemically imbalanced, or brimming with the feeling that they were wronged in some way, either by an individual or individuals or by society. Many slipped through cracks in the system. When one backtracks, one often can see that there were indications all along. For example, when Winston went from sating his thirst for blood by killing rabbits to cats and dogs, his neighbors complained to the police. But they did nothing; and as a consequence, he became emboldened and graduated to *Homo sapiens*."

Mahakavi tapped the top of the case. "From here down to there"—he swept his hand to the right—"are the rank amateurs. Like Winston, they lacked ingenuity. They were impulsive. Over there, if you're interested, I have some marvelous artifacts from The Horoscope Killer, who stymied police for ten years. I also bought the Bible owned by the Mad Monk. He terrorized religious leaders across the state for two years. And in that display case over there, I have the client list of the prostitute Gwendolyn, one of the few female serial killers."

"Do you have any"—she searched for the right word—"collectibles from Sean Strickland?"

Mahakavi was jittery. At first, Summer thought he was ill, but then realized he was laughing silently. "Sean fits into the amateur category, although he certainly held delusions of being one of the grand men of serial murder. Of course, he did manage to kill four men involved in law enforcement, and that is no easy task, but really, when you get down to it, he lacked imagination."

"Why did Strickland kill law enforcement?"

"Sean believed he was the ultimate law. He felt he had to destroy the law in order to promote his own law."

"What law was that?"

"He didn't say."

"What about the marks he left on the victims' backs?"

Summer watched Mahakavi's toes curl in his sandals. "I can see you are a fan of the genre. What was your name again?"

"Summer."

"Ah, yes. At the time, the police were unable to decipher the mark—not marks, which was a popular misconception. When Strickland perished, they simply closed the case. But subsequently I was able to determine its meaning."

"And?"

"*Om.*"

"What?"

"The lines he drew on his victims' skin represent the Hindu symbol *Om*, which is used in chants, particularly in Buddhism. It is a mantra used in contemplating the ultimate reality—oneness with the universe. But Sean didn't render it correctly. Come with me."

Summer moved down the row of cases with Mahakavi, who stopped at a case containing a sheet of paper with two sets of squiggly lines, side by side. "The symbol on the right is a copy of the symbol Strickland drew on his victims. The one on the left is the correct rendition of *Om*. As you can see, they are identical, except for the line on the bottom right that twists incorrectly."

And both, Summer noted, were similar, though not identical, to the mark on Gundy's back.

"Strickland was strictly a thug," Mahakavi said. "Why on earth would you be interested in him?"

"My father was the investigator on the case."

"You are Wib Neuwirth's daughter?" Mahakavi's face beamed. "This is certainly an honor. He is retired now?"

"He died six months ago."

"Oh? I am sorry for your loss."

Summer offered a perfunctory "Thank you."

"At last, I will be able to close Sean's file. Detective Neuwirth was the last one."

"Last what?"

Mahakavi acted surprised that Summer didn't know. "Why, the last person involved in the Strickland case to die."

Summer jammed her hands under her armpits. She was cold. Mahakavi kept the temperature regulated to protect his collection. "Can I see the letter from Strickland to my father that you bought at auction?"

Two cases down, a letter was tacked inside, a stamped envelope (no return address) perched on a stand next to it. An auctioneer's certificate of authenticity was posted behind it.

The letter was composed of letters cut out of magazines, books, and newspapers, glued to the paper:

NEUwIRTH YOUR NEXT.
THEN YoUR FAMILY.
SEAN STRICKLANd.

Mahakavi sucked his front teeth. "Notice how he spelled the first 'you're'?' Sean was never one to pay attention to details."

Summer remembered the moment Wib opened the note, the worry that etched his face, the way his breathing became more focused, more labored, fear for his family driving blood through his heart. She flashed to the moment that had haunted her through her teens—when, on a misty night, Strickland had broken into their home through Summer's window. She awoke to see Strickland's lean face, hair plastered to his skull, his eyes dull and bloodshot.

She screamed and Wib came running, gun drawn. Then an explosion of gunfire as Wib shot at Strickland, who took off across the yard. The start of a nightmare that didn't end until Wib took off in hot pursuit, tires hydroplaning on the twisting road, and drove Strickland off the side of a mountain, where Strickland had died in a fiery ball.

Unless he hadn't.

Summer studied the letter, the cracked and yellowing paper. *If* Strickland were alive and carrying on his vendetta, Gundy might not be the only one to end up with his skull crushed, a lipstick calling card scrawled on his back. She could be next.

Summer superimposed her memory of Strickland with the face of Marsalis. Both must have been born around the same time, were staple-thin, unkempt, reptilian in speech and manner, insane. What if they were the same man?

Summer realized the collector was talking to her. "What?"

Mahakavi was pointing to his phone. "I *said*, would you mind if I took your picture? I would like to add it to the archive. After all, it is not every day the daughter of the investigating officer of a serial murderer visits me."

CHAPTER 12

SUMMER DIDN'T RETURN HOME until dusk, a violet-gilded sunset. She stopped to listen to the crickets and the wheeze of insects, like the noise that had been ringing in her ears at work. Habit prevented her from taking out her keys until she was sure no one lurked.

The windows of her apartment were clammed shut, the air inside dead and still. She flipped on the light. She moved furtively, unsure of where Marsalis's surveillance cameras were placed or what he could see. She had decided to avoid compromising positions. She changed clothes by hanging a blanket over her head. Only made calls from throwaway cell phones, which she quickly discarded. Didn't bring office paperwork home.

When she passed by her computer monitor, she jumped back. Marsalis's face shone onscreen. Large letters underneath: *Answers to your questions, but first, answers to my questions.* Then an Internet address.

She backed away, as if the machine could infect her, and paced her apartment until she calmed down. She felt weak, her stomach all growly, and realized she hadn't eaten all day. She pulled a box of cereal out of the pantry and stuffed Cheerios in her mouth, spilling crumbs on the floor; put the box back, realized she was still hungry, munched some more, put the box back; then finished it off and tossed the empty box into the trash.

When she wasn't shaky anymore, she sat down and faced the monitor.

She logged on. Marsalis had clearly juiced up her computer with more RAM, speed, a faster modem, and software that could download full-motion video and stereo sound.

She typed in the address Marsalis had left her, and the software spirited her through cyberspace to a homepage plastered with a photo of herself. A banner underneath said, *Click here, Summer*. When she did, she was faced with a conundrum.

The answers are the passwords. Without the passwords, you will be denied the answers you seek.

What answers? she wondered. About Sonia, Wib, Strickland, the existence of the video of Gundy's murder? Or were these answers to questions Summer hadn't even thought of?

It was a test. She answered basic questions like date of birth, year of high school graduation, college graduation, law class ranking. Then the questions got more personal: form of birth control, favorite sexual position, the name of the last man she'd spent the night with.

When she lied (or forgot), the computer chastised her and wouldn't let her go on.

Summer's hands were sweaty; her fingers slipped on the mouse. She was on a scavenger hunt for her life. But to learn what Marsalis knew meant she had to play his game.

Now she was on a site labeled *Summer's Big Secrets*. Ringing the edge of the screen were miniature banners, actual documents, certificates, letters, news stories—all details obscured.

Choose one. Summer clicked on an official-looking document affixed with the icon "Sonia's Crime," and the screen flowered.

But instead of answers, more questions.

What time of day were you accosted?

Summer crashed her fist into the keyboard. *gbmgyg*, the screen read.

Data error.

Fuck you, Marsalis. She hit "return."

Data error. One more incorrect answer and this session will be terminated.

Summer couldn't face not knowing about Sonia. What crime? Was this the reason her mother had vanished? Shaking from the cold and the fact that Marsalis had her psyche on the rack, Summer typed, *Dusk.*

The weapon?

A knife, lodged under my chin.

From which direction did the attacker approach?

Behind.

What did he do next?

Why are you doing this to me?

Data error.

He forced me inside.

Then?

He wrapped duct tape around my face so I couldn't identify him.

What did he do next?

He beat me, and tied my hands up with more tape.

Then?

Sliced off my clothes with the knife.

What else?

He heated the blade of the knife on the stove and burned my back.

Did you beg him to stop?

Yes.

What did he do next?

Summer yanked at her hair. She didn't know how much more she could take.

Unless you respond within 10 seconds, this session will be terminated. 9-8-7-6-5-

He raped me, OK?

Did it hurt?

She had worked so hard to blot out these memories. She stood up, walked away. When she looked back at the screen, the count was on. *4-3-2-*

She typed: *Yes, it hurt.*

When he was done, what did he do?

Summer was beyond pain now. *He urinated on me.*

Then what?

He doused me with bathroom cleaner, to mask the urine in case the crime lab tried to analyze it.

Before he left, what did he say?

"Don't worry, bitch, I used a condom."

And?

Told me he should have cut me up.

Were you lucky?

I'm still alive.

But inside you died just a little bit?

You're a bastard, Marsalis.

Data error.

When her time was almost up and everything she'd just gone through might be for naught, she gave in. *Yes.*

She was trembling. The memory of the rape tearing her up inside, the pain, humiliation, all of it pushed into the front of her mind. A tear dripped on the keyboard.

The screen grew into full-frame. "Congratulations, Summer!" Marsalis's recorded voice. "Your reward for successfully completing this examination is information. What you choose to do with it is entirely your affair."

A death certificate for a four-year old child hovered in the middle of the screen. Her eyes settled on the name.

Summer Neuwirth.

PART III

UNREASONABLE DOUBTS

CHAPTER 13

SUMMER WAS IN THE OFFICE EARLY, breakfast having consisted of a gin-soaked olive. Levi was already there, in the computer room. Summer peered over his shoulder. He was surfing the net. Summer could barely watch.

Levi glanced up, then immediately looked away. "You look like hell."

"I've been having trouble sleeping," she said. "What're you looking for?"

"Information on the appeals process for death penalty cases. I want to make sure I have updated information."

"SK may thank you for this."

Levi shrugged. When he clicked, the screen froze. "Shit. That's the third time. Must be all the pirated software we run. I half-expect the D.A. to bust down the door and indict us all."

Levi shut the machine off and rebooted. "I'd tell you to go home and get some sleep, but since we're so short-staffed, how about a Tic Tac?"

"No, thanks."

"What's the latest on SK?"

"Get this," Summer said. "Gundy's place was wired for surveillance. Raines told me the cops found hidden cameras all over the place hooked up to a computer."

"Hmm. Well, don't sweat it until we know for sure it's not Gundy's private porn habit run amok." Levi chewed on his pinky nail. "I have some news that should cheer you up. I got SK moved to a new cell. Five-fucking-stars, compared to the last one."

Summer smiled and took a seat. "Is it our anniversary?"

"Let's just say the warden's son got into trouble once and I helped smooth things," Levi said in his usual off-handed way. "But there was a tradeoff. You won't be able to visit SK in her cell; it'll have to be between glass. He can't look like he's backing down because of political pressure, so he's by the book on this one."

"I'm sure SK won't mind. What do you think of Hightower being assigned the case?"

"I'd say that next to Judge Kelly, it was the last thing you wanted. But not a lot we could have done about it."

"Raines wins either way."

"Yeah, but all's not lost. Hightower's up for re-election, and guess who's running against him in the primary?"

"Raines?"

Levi slapped the side of the monitor and it flashed to life. "How'd you know? It's been a more tightly kept secret than Coke's formula."

"Tai told me."

Levi grinned. "I must say, he has his ear to the ground. Anyway, I'm sure they'll both pander shamelessly to the media, but they'll also be on their best behavior. If you make a motion, you can be sure Hightower will ponder it rather than rejecting it out of hand just because it comes from the defense."

"Maybe." The thought of doing battle with Raines in Hightower's court brought on a surge of adrenaline. She dropped her files and books on the floor, and suddenly felt a razor-sharp pain on her finger. She was bleeding. "Shit. A paper cut," she said, sticking her finger in her mouth.

"Band-Aids are in my desk," Levi said, getting back to the computer.

Holding her finger aloft, Summer went into Levi's office and sifted through his desk drawer. After wrapping her finger up and stanching the blood flow, she noticed a stack of photos rubber banded together, the top one of the office Christmas party: Summer, Rosie, and Levi, drunk and red-eyed from the flash, falling over, arms around one another's shoulders.

The memory made her sad.

CHAPTER 14

SUMMER WAS FACING SK, plexiglass between them. She picked up the phone. SK followed suit. They stared at each other, static over the line. Summer could hear other jailhouse conversations, other languages, around her.

"You're welcome for getting you a new cell," Summer said finally.

SK remained quiet, her angry eyes locked on Summer.

Summer continued, "I haven't received any notification, so I assume you haven't tried to Marsden me yet."

"You said it yourself," SK said. "Even if I did try to Marsden you, it's nearly impossible to remove an attorney."

"Then let's get down to business." Summer wrestled with the urge to make a clean break. Speaking through pursed lips, she said, "I'm curious about the boot. How did glass and blood get on it?"

"I've been wondering that myself."

"What happened during the search of your residence?"

"I'm not sure. I got home in the middle of it."

"How many cops were there?"

"About half a dozen."

"Were they paired up or working solo?"

"Some solo, some in teams."

"What about Detective Tyler?"

"I don't now. Fifteen minutes after I walked in, he told me I was under arrest for the murder of Harold Gundy."

"And you just bolted?"

"I panicked," SK said defensively. "I saw an open window and jumped through. Then I just ran."

"The boots, they *are* yours, right?"

"Yes."

"You told me you dropped off the pictures of your late husband at Gundy's. When?"

"The afternoon he was murdered."

Summer covered her mouth with her hand, then removed it. "That could account for your fingerprints on the outside of the door and on the pictures. But if the D.A. shows you visited Gundy's the day he was murdered, a jury is likely to convict you."

"Not if I take the stand and explain."

Summer shook her head. "You have priors for prostitution. That would be big trouble if you testify."

SK cocked her head. "I thought they weren't allowed to bring up convictions for crimes not related to the one you're being tried for."

"Except these are what they call 'crimes of moral turpitude.' You get on the stand, the D.A. will roast you alive."

"I'm taking the stand."

"We'll talk about it later." Summer knew when to duck.

"I'll find a way to make sure the jury hears about all the wonderful things you've done for the community, the childcare center, rape-crisis hot line, the hostel for battered women—"

"But not the dojo?"

"Oh, I'm sure the D.A. will mention that."

"How do you think I paid for it all?" SK said edgily. "From working as a stripper and a prostitute. I figured the way to bury my sins was to improve the plight of women."

"I'm curious. What made you change?"

SK drew her hair into a ponytail and knotted it to get it out of her eyes. "Business was great for a while, and I was making a ton of money, but then the Haze County cops ran me out of town. Then in New York I was raped. And the cops' view was like, Hey, you're a fucking whore, so if some guy goes for a little bonus nookie, why not?"

Summer flashed to her own rape.

"I didn't see him until it was too late," SK continued. "He pulled a gun on me right outside my building, told me to take him past the doorman and up to my apartment. He terrorized me for eight hours. I thought he was going to kill me."

Summer peered through the barrier at SK, separated by glass and years but not experiences. "That's the worst part," Summer said distantly. "Not knowing whether he's going to kill you or not. Afterward, I wondered if I would have been better off if he had. These bastards use sex as a weapon, they take away our security. I thought of killing myself after—"

SK was staring.

Summer dropped the phone. It clattered. Trying not to totally fall apart, she ran out of the room, didn't stop until she had gotten to the prison parking lot, where she picked up her truck and gunned it to the office.

Safely inside, her door shut, she murmured, "Fuck! Fuck! Fuck!" in a mantra. She had blown it. SK would never retain a lawyer who couldn't keep herself together. She wondered why she didn't feel relieved.

Rosie opened the door, then knocked. "What's going on?"

"Nothing," Summer said. "Been one of those kinds of days."

Rosie laughed. "Usually I'm the one losing her shit."

Summer needed Rosie, needed to lean on her, but was afraid to put herself out on a limb.

Rosie kept her distance, staying in the hall. "Are you all right?"

Summer wanted to let it all pour out, but knew if she did, she would never be able to put it back. "I'm OK. Thanks."

"Good, good. Listen, one of my clients, a prostitute, was busted for possession and intent to sell. She said to give this to SK's attorney. That's you, right?" Rosie handed her an envelope.

Summer resisted the urge to tell Rosie to keep it for herself—or pass it on to Brockton. "What's a B-girl want with me?"

"She didn't say."

"What's her name?"

"Melba Ignacio."

It didn't strike a chord.

"Can I ask you something, Rosie?"

"Maybe."

As in, not if it has to do with us, Summer realized. *Fine.* "What do you know about Tai Sanborn?"

Rosie was caught off guard, but quickly righted herself. "Besides that he's half-Japanese and so fine he could be modeling underwear? Only that the cops hate him. The story goes some of the boys were skimming crack from the drug lab and then reselling it. When Sanborn got wind, he bled it to internal affairs. They reassigned him to another division, but not for long. He was chasing this perp into a crack house when his partner ran out of there like a candy-assed baboon. The perp winged him."

"Where was he hit?"

"His gun hand."

"So that spelled the end of his cop days?"

"You can't be a cop if you can't shoot straight."

"How do you know all this?"

Rosie blew on her fingernails and brushed them against her chest. "Who do you think defended the perp?"

Rosie returned to her office. Seconds later, Summer's phone rang. She picked up.

"Just so you know," Rosie said, "I got him a real good deal, too." Click.

Smiling, Summer hung up and tore open the letter from Ignacio. The handwriting was flowery and adolescent, a bubble dot over the 'i.'

I saw who killed Gundy.

CHAPTER 15

THE SUN PEERED OVER KNOBBY MOUNTAINS, casting oblique shadows around the parched tombstones. Two burly men in windbreakers, the faded logo of the Haze County Medical Examiner's office on their backs, were thigh-deep in the earth, shoveling dirt. There was a numb clank when metal struck coffin.

Summer was sitting on a headstone flipped sideways. Between dangling legs, she could read part of the epitaph: *Sean Alvin Strickland. March 1, 1949 - May 24, 19—*. Spray-painted profanity covered the rest, but she knew when he was supposed to have died. It was amazing, Summer reflected, how few people could spell "Satan."

One of the diggers scrambled out of the ground and up to a crane while the other donned gloves and swept dirt from the top of the coffin. Summer wondered what Strickland's victims would say to his unburying. If she tried hard enough, could she hear their diphthongs of grief and rage?

"Hey," Chantelle N'Dour, the medical examiner, said,

handing Summer coffee in Styrofoam. "I'm just in time for the tricky part."

West African by birth, American by choice, Chantelle was a wet-dream witness for the D.A.: intelligent, well-prepared, and her science was beyond reproach. White jurors, always the majority in Haze County, convinced themselves they weren't racist by giving Chantelle's testimony extra weight. Summer had cross-examined her many times, knew that Chantelle was as beautiful and brilliant as she was statuesque—6'2", all bone and moonless-night complexion.

Summer sipped coffee. "What's tricky about lifting a coffin out of the ground?"

"You mean raising the dead? He's been in the ground a long time—" She shouted at the gloved digger, who was fumbling with cable. "Make sure you triple the straps, Boyd. We don't want Mr. Strickland's remains to tumble out."

Summer detected a hodgepodge of accents: African, French, British, and New Jersey, where Chantelle had studied for her doctorate.

Boyd yelled back. "Yeah, yeah. I'll make you a deal, Chan. The guy falls out, treat me like your ancestors would."

"How's that?"

"Throw me in a pot of boiling water and serve me as soup."

Chantelle laughed. "You can eat me, too, Boyd."

Summer envied how easily she got along with men.

Chantelle plucked at her blouse, fanning her chest with the material. "I can't believe how fucking hot it is, and it's only dawn."

"Isn't West Africa hot?" Summer asked.

"Not this hot," Chantelle said. "How did you keep the press away?"

"The last thing Raines wants is a media shower. Did you bring breakfast?"

"Like I promised." Chantelle reached into a paper bag and handed Summer a bagel. "What does this exhumation have to do with the demise of Mr. Gundy?"

Summer unwrapped the bagel, licked the cream cheese oozing out of the side, and took a bite. Chewing, she said, "Everything, nothing. I'll let you know after you tell me what you find out. For now, I just want to know if the guy in that coffin really is Sean Strickland."

"You think it's possible it's not?"

"If I didn't, I wouldn't be here on my day off."

Boyd finished wrapping up the coffin and grunted his way out of the pit.

Chantelle edged off the tombstone. "Come on."

Summer joined Chantelle, their toes brushing the grave's edge. The other digger cranked up the crane.

"Wait!" Chantelle skimmed the side of her hand against her throat. When the crane stopped, she said, "Boyd? Where's the tarp? If this coffin breaks apart, I want to make sure that we catch all of whatever is left of the dearly departed."

Boyd threw up his hands like he was curling dumbbells. He took off for the parking lot.

"While we're waiting, can I ask you some questions?" Summer asked.

Watching Boyd, Chantelle said, "It's a free country."

"If the killer hadn't smashed Gundy with the bottle, would he have died anyway from the fall?"

"Oh, those kinds of questions. Hard to say. You want my opinion?"

"Is anybody else around here qualified to answer?"

"No one alive." Chantelle's expression soured as Boyd returned, dragging a tarp. "Boyd," she yelled, "what the hell are you doing, man? I've got to run tests on the body. I don't want to chance excess contamination."

Even from 50 feet away, Summer could hear Boyd sigh. "I've been digging graves and digging up bodies for twenty years, missy," he yelled back. "The guy ain't coming out of no coffin. It's pine. Solid."

"He'd better not," Chantelle mumbled.

Boyd gathered up the tarp in his arms, made sure no ends trailed on the ground, and continued toward Strickland's grave.

"Would he have?" Summer asked. "And keep it sub-Ph.D."

"You don't want to know all the science, right? Just the stuff that will either help or hurt your client," Chantelle said, staring down Boyd.

"Of course," Summer said.

"Typical lawyer." Chantelle cupped her hands in a makeshift megaphone. "Boyd, already dirt has rolled onto the tarp. We can't have old dirt mixing with new dirt."

Boyd muttered, audible but indecipherable. He shook off the tarp and lowered it into the hole; the tarp roll ended up kissing the coffin.

"I'm not sure whether the victim died before being hit on the head or not. But he would have died from the fall no matter what, unless he'd received prompt medical care," Chantelle said.

Summer nodded. "In the ME report, it says the time of death was between ten and twelve. How do you know?"

"Gundy was stiff from the waist down when he was found. Rigor mortis travels from head to foot and exits the same way."

"What else can you tell me?"

"The lack level of swelling around his injuries, including several broken bones, indicates he died in perhaps as little as a few seconds, perhaps as much as a ten minutes, after suffering these injuries. As for the damage to his skull, I'm not sure when that happened yet."

Summer pictured Raines on his knees in front of the jury, starring in Gundy's final role: an innocent victim pleading for mercy. "What else?"

"The killer was right-handed."

"So are most people. Did you find my client's fingerprints inside the condo?"

"Ask the cops. I don't do windows and I don't do fingerprints—unless I'm ID-ing a body."

"What about hair fibers?"

"From your client?"

"Yes."

"Curiously, no."

Summer had read the report but was glad to hear it confirmed. "How about other hair fibers?"

"Lots." Chantelle giggled. "Apparently, our Mr. Gundy entertained frequently."

"Male, female?"

"You know we cannot ascertain gender from hair fibers."

"What about dyes, shampoos? Can't that be an indication?"

"These days, boys act like girls, girls act like boys."

"What kind of hair are we talking about? Blond? Brunette? Redhead? Anyone dye their hair?"

"All of the above."

"Really? He did entertain a lot. Clothing fibers?"

"From your client? The police didn't bring me any."

"How are you going to testify with regards to the murder?"

"I'll tell what I know. That judging from his internal injuries, Mr. Gundy was either kicked or thrown from the second floor and hit glass. He suffered massive hematoma, damaged kidneys, a broken spleen, and cracked ribs. He was also struck repeatedly on the back of his head with a blunt instrument: the bottle. When I complete the toxicology tests, I'll have a better idea of what exactly killed him."

"Anything special about the lipstick?"

"You can buy it at any cosmetics counter."

The crane cranked to life again, gears grinding, straps straining. As the coffin rose, Boyd spread the tarp underneath. It was brought to rest a few feet from Chantelle.

"Should we take a peek?" Summer asked, half-serious.

"Trust me," Chantelle said. "Not a good idea after eating cream cheese."

After winding their way through tombstones, Chantelle and Summer waited by the truck while Boyd and his co-digger transported the coffin over.

Chantelle glanced at Strickland's autopsy report. "I don't understand how you expect me to confirm Mr. Strickland's death without something to compare him to. No fingerprints—hell, no *fingers* left. No head or teeth either, so forget about comparing the remains to his dental records, even if we could locate those."

"Check the DNA against this." Summer handed Chantelle the letter Strickland had sent to Wib. It had taken a subpoena, and Mahakavi had been none too happy about it.

"What's this?" Chantelle asked after Summer showed her what was written. "You want me to look for fingerprints on the paper? Did he sign it in blood?"

Summer pressed on. "He must have licked the stamp and the envelope closed. I want you to analyze his saliva. It must be there mixed in with the glue."

"That's crazy."

"If archaeologists can use DNA analysis to identify 4000-year-old mummies, you should have no problem," Summer said.

"I'm no archaeologist—OK, OK," Chantelle said, pre-empting Summer. "How do you know we'll find anything?"

"Strickland was no germ freak. He must have licked the stamp and the envelope to seal it. And why wouldn't he? They didn't have DNA analysis in his heyday."

The diggers, bearing the coffin, approached in the wasted light of morning. Summer watched as they stowed the coffin in the back of her truck.

Boyd smirked as he handed Chantelle a clipboard. "I told you, Chan," he said. "Maybe you got these university degrees, but I know coffins."

Chantelle checked her watch, filled in the time. "You win this time, Boyd. Tell you what: I'll buy the first round at Kelly's."

"After work?"

Chantelle signed the paperwork with a flourish. "Sure."

After Boyd and his partner left, Chantelle double-checked the lock, and then told Summer, "I am officially intrigued. I look forward to seeing you in court."

Summer rolled her shoulders to get the kinks out. "Why shouldn't you? Last time you clobbered me."

"Your client clobbered you," Chantelle reminded her. "I merely handed him the club."

A felony assault case. Summer's client had engaged a woman at a bar, led her outside, and almost killed her, crushing her clavicle, pelvis, and nose. No witnesses, but Chantelle discovered unique fibers on the victim's clothes, which turned out to be station wagon carpeting. It had taken weeks, but she tracked them to a Ford manufactured three decades earlier; only five still ran in the whole state, including one belonging to Summer's client.

"Need a lift?" Chantelle asked.

"Brought my bike," Summer said.

"I was wondering why you were wearing such tight shorts." Chantelle ducked into the driver's side. Shut the door and rolled down the window. "I'll send over a report soon as I've got something."

Summer leaned into the window. "Can I ask you a question a little out of your area of expertise? Recently, I was checking on a death certificate. Even though I had the name and registration number, the Town Hall copy was missing."

"This related to Gundy?"

Summer peered heavenward and whistled softly.

"Message received," Chantelle said. "If you already have a copy, why do you need another?"

"To see if it had been faked."

"How far back are we talking?"

"Almost 25 years."

"Hah!" Chantelle hee-hawed. "Haze County bureaucracy is specially designed to lose paper. A clerk could have misfiled it."

"And I'd never find it. Any other possibilities?"

"Someone could have bribed a clerk."

"Why?"

"The county doesn't have the manpower or technical savvy to cross-reference birth certificates and death certificates, and the records aren't computerized. That would make too much sense. If someone wanted to assume a new identity, all he'd have to do is find someone around the same age who died. Anyone with access to newspaper archives—birth announcements, obituaries—could do this."

Summer cricked her neck. "Then what?"

Chantelle checked her lipstick in the mirror. "You planning on assuming a new identity?"

"I already have. You see, I'm really a man. Could some guy acquire a new birth certificate?"

"And social security card, passport, driver's license. Hell, not only could he inherit your credit history, he could actually take over your identity." Chantelle gunned the engine. "Information can be a very scary thing."

The van shook. Summer's elbows tingled. She backed up and waved.

Chantelle drove away.

Summer unlocked her bike. Out of the corner of her eye, she saw a deep-blue van squeal into the parking lot. She thought it was a TV news crew, until it came straight at her. She was about to dive out of the way when, broadside, the van skidded to a stop.

She grabbed her pump. Her heart jackhammered. She noticed that her knuckles were white under her bike gloves.

The door slid open.

Marsalis gestured inside to dazzling lights and sparkling high-tech—computer monitors, scanners, video screens, music mixer—and sang, "Fly me to the moon."

CHAPTER 16

MARSALIS COMPLETED HIS *a cappella* half-chorus and stepped out of the van.

Summer brandished the pump.

He stopped and held up his hands. "Please, sir, don't hurt me," he said in a little girl's voice.

Summer gripped the pump tighter. "What do you want?"

"If you get in, I'll take you to Sonia."

"I'm not getting into that car with you."

He shuffled closer. "Not even if I can show you proof of her whereabouts?"

Summer backed away, putting her bike between her and him. "I'm warning you. Stay away from me."

Marsalis dismissed her with a wave of his hand and returned to the van. He opened the passenger-side door and grabbed a legal-sized envelope. Holding the corner with two fingers, he rocked it back and forth. "Come and get it."

"No."

Marsalis sighed. "You're no fun." He flicked the envelope to Summer and climbed inside the van.

Keeping one eye on Marsalis, Summer slid the contents onto the asphalt: an article from the *Haze County Register*, from more than two decades before; yellowed paper held together with crinkly tape.

When Summer read the news brief, her eyes saucered: A four-year-old girl drowned yesterday in—the name of the lake was blacked out—marking the first tourist-industry related death in the town's history.

> *Shortly after lunch, Summer Neuwirth was playing unattended by the edge of the lake. By the time Sonia Neuwirth noticed that her four-year-old daughter was missing, it was too late.*
>
> *It took divers several hours to locate the body. But police were confident that they had been searching the right place after they scooped the child's doll out of the water.*
>
> *One police officer investigating the case, who insisted on anonymity, said Mrs. Neuwirth may have been inebriated when her child disappeared. "It's a shame, really. The woman was celebrating her anniversary with her husband and this happens," he said.*
>
> *A spokesman for the District Attorney's office said it was doubtful that charges would be filed.*

Summer re-read the account twice. She was startled by a car horn.

"Bummer, huh?" Marsalis called.

"I don't believe it."

"Picture this: Sonia, Wib, and their only child. Sonia and Wib are celebrating their anniversary, but they have an argument. Wib stalks off. You know how Sonia drove him mad."

"No."

"Sonia is upset. This is not what she had planned at all for her anniversary. So she drinks, like she always does when she's depressed. Maybe she passes out. Her daughter wanders off, plays near the water. The police found the doll first, so I assume she'd lost it in the water. When she tried to liberate it, she fell in. Drowned. Can you imagine what it must have felt like when the water began to choke her, the delicious terror she must have experienced?"

Summer's stomach burned. "I'd know if I were adopted."

"Who said you were adopted?"

"What's all this about?"

Marsalis coughed. "Why don't you ask Sonia?"

"I would if I could."

"Then get in. I'll take you to her."

Summer looked at Marsalis, then the newspaper clipping, then at Marsalis again. "Why don't you just tell me where she is?"

"Either pay my price or the deal is off."

"How do I know this newspaper article is real? How do I know you didn't doctor it?"

"You don't."

"I'm not getting into that van with you, Marsalis."

"Suit yourself." He reached over and pulled the passenger-side door shut, then revved the engine.

Summer watched him drive to the exit, put his turn signal on, and wait for traffic to thin. She skimmed the article one more time. She visualized Sonia and Wib and this little girl who shared her name at this lake. What if Marsalis hadn't concocted this just to rattle her? The rims of her ears burned. Before she realized what she was doing, she began waving and shouting.

Marsalis backed the van into the parking lot.

Summer loaded her bike and climbed aboard. She sat with her fists clenched, waiting for Marsalis to make a move.

"Buckle up," he said.

"Where are we going?"

"You'll see."

They drove in silence for a while, Summer watching the countryside change from desert to lush, up into the mountains where they hit cloud cover. Outside, it began to rain, first reluctantly, then in sheets.

When Summer bent down to pull up her socks, she noticed a gun lodged under Marsalis's seat.

She kept her tone conversational. "How did you know where to find me?"

"I always know where to find you," he said. "But I'm often disappointed. You expend a great deal of energy trying not to reveal yourself to me, Summer. When you are home, you find creative ways not to show me your beauty. You hide under fabrics and blankets."

"You hide behind a cloak of mystery and terror yourself. Why are you stalking me?"

"Even before you met me, I knew you. Like a mother is always with her child, even when separated by years or events, I knew I would always be with you, until the day you die."

"That sounds ethereal for a man who earns his living in the rational world of computing."

"Some phenomena are hard to explain. Like the fact that I have never caught you masturbating at home. Did the rape scare you from having sex, even alone?"

"Shut up, Marsalis."

He gave her a wheezy snicker. "Actually, judging by your behavior, you are more infomaniac than nymphomaniac. Does it bother you that Sonia ran away from you?"

Summer tensed. "Maybe she had a good reason."

"Would you find any reason satisfactory?"

Summer answered honestly. "No."

"Sonia was very disappointed in you."

"That's not true. Sonia was sick. She didn't have complete control of her faculties after Wib died."

"Did you provide her with the best care possible?"

"I did my best."

"Your best?" Marsalis looked at her with incredulous eyes as he drove, his hands gripping the steering wheel. "Where were you when she underwent her first chemotherapy session and needed a ride from the hospital?"

"I had a trial."

"When she returned home, she would call your name for hours, sobbing out of control. But no one was there to listen. Only after she disappeared did you miss her."

"Pull over. I'm getting out."

"Ever since Sonia disappeared, there's been a hole in your life. But don't you realize that you dug a hole for Sonia that was even deeper?"

Summer struggled with the door, but only Marsalis could unlock it.

"You drove her away," he continued. "She couldn't bear to live out her final days on earth with you. She preferred to spend them with someone else."

The seat belt dug into her shoulder when Summer leaned over. She had to strain to reach the gun under Marsalis's seat.

With a final lunge, she was able to snatch it. She poked him in the ear with the barrel.

"Stop the car," she ordered.

Marsalis wiggled his tongue at her, and then floored it. The speedometer read 75, 90, 100. Marsalis slalomed through traffic. Over the groan of the engine he hissed, "Is the joy you would feel killing me worth dying for?"

Summer tugged on the trigger. The chamber flicked forward one sixteenth of a turn.

Marsalis added speed: 110, 120, 125. Two cars collided behind.

Summer considered the weight of the gun in her hand. She pushed the gun harder into Marsalis's temple. "I said, 'Stop the car.'"

"Shoot me."

"Stop the car!" Louder this time.

"Fuck you!"

Summer shouted, "Stop-the-car-you-misogynistic-cyber-geek-psychopath—"

Marsalis joined in, merrily screeching while weaving through traffic.

Summer pulled the trigger.

Click.

Marsalis sputtered. One part laugh, one part cough.

Summer shot him again. Nothing.

He pulled the gun to his mouth and puckered his lips around the barrel. Summer squeezed the trigger, felt the spring action load. But no bullet. Not even a blank.

Marsalis spat out the gun. "Tastes like rust."

Summer fired at Marsalis's profile. He slumped forward, clutched his heart, shut his eyes, but continued steering. He sprang to life. "No bullets. Satisfied?"

"There are two shots left." Again, Summer pulled the trigger.

This time Marsalis flinched. He veered into the opposing lane; a truck, horn blaring, hurtled at them. When Summer braced for impact, Marsalis grabbed the barrel of the gun and torqued the steering wheel. They swerved back into their own lane.

They wrestled for the gun, Marsalis straining to direct the barrel away from his head. They were doing a steady 120. They squirted between two trucks, passing them like they were going backward.

Summer squeezed the trigger and fought the gun's recoil. There was a tremendous explosion as the driver's side window shattered, showering them with glass. Wind whistled inside the car.

Marsalis let go of the barrel and rode the brake, slowing to 55. They passed a road sign. Next right: *Fayres 10 miles, St. Freeburgh 12 miles, Redwood Falls 26 miles.* They were at Haze County's northern edge. Marsalis was breathing rapidly, sweat prickling on his forehead. After wiping her prints, Summer tossed the gun into the back.

They were silent until the turn off, and then Marsalis said, "There's glass in your leg, from the window."

Summer plucked a fragment out of her shorts.

"You figured out it was a test," Marsalis said.

"It wasn't your first."

"How did you know there was only one bullet?"

"The heft of the gun." Summer looked out onto the moving landscape, the vineyards bursting purple, ice-capped mountains, a pack of deer. Here, over the Santa Ana Range, it was cool and lush.

Marsalis brushed errant glass off the dashboard. "Wib taught you to shoot?"

"He gave me a gun for my Sweet Sixteen."

"How did you know the last chamber held the only bullet?"

She shrugged. "I knew you wouldn't leave anything to chance."

Marsalis took the turn to Fayres. "I'm curious as to what you're feeling right now."

Summer hid behind a mask of impassivity.

Marsalis continued, "But curiosity can get you into trouble, or endanger others. Take Jimi Cruz."

"How does Jimi Cruz pose a danger to you?"

"To *you*."

"What are you talking about?"

"I know you don't watch much TV, but tune into Channel 54 tomorrow, a cable-access show of mine that debuts at 3:30 a.m. I have a wonderful surprise for you." Marsalis ungripped the wheel and posed: Two thumbs up.

"What have you done to Jimi Cruz?" she asked.

Marsalis was back on the wheel. "Tune in tomorrow."

Summer tried to put the puzzle together, but there weren't enough pieces. She knew of no strategy that would force Marsalis to give her what she wanted. He had a drug dealer way about him: He made himself indispensible; then, after hooking her, pressed his advantage. All she could do was wait him out.

They passed a sign for a lakefront resort.

"Enough about Jimi Cruz," Marsalis said. "Let's talk about Sonia."

Summer fidgeted with her seat belt. "Sure."

Marsalis parked near the lake, the town's tourist magnet. A short distance away, there was a resort, restaurants, cafés, a bookstore, and shops bursting with kitsch. The lake shimmered emerald. Tourists meandered along the water's edge.

"Right off there"—Marsalis pointed out a spot on the path running along the lake—"is where the doll and the child's corpse were found." Marsalis reached across Summer's body and opened her door. "Sonia's *wait*ing," he crooned.

Summer continued to sit in shocked stillness, but Marsalis insisted, flicking her shoulder with his fingers. She got out of the car, her knees crackling. She looked around, wary of her new freedom. But Marsalis took care of that when he slammed the door shut and, kicking up gravel, peeled out.

After she watched Marsalis shrink to a crumb on the horizon, Summer took the path to the water and skirted the edge. She surveyed the terrain. The banks were slippery, few vines to hang onto. A snake sunned itself on a log. Cattails grew in the muck. The scent of skunk cabbage. Summer tried to visualize what must have happened. The girl must have slid through those cattails.

With mincing steps, she approached the water. Below the surface was a doll, tethered off shore. Another Marsalis prop, she thought. She leaned over for a better look when her footing gave way. She slipped, flailing in the mud, and pitched headfirst into glacier-fed water. After adjusting to the icy shock, she treaded over to the doll. She untethered it and tossed it up on the bank. Relying on vines jutting out of the mud, she pulled herself up to land. Sopping wet, she stood on the shore—stared at the doll, studied the water.

The doll was filthy and waterlogged, one of its eyes popped out. Summer remembered when and where she had last seen it: As a teenager she had rifled through one of her mother's closets, looking for a special pair of shoes, when she came across a box holding an old doll wrapped in tissue paper.

When Sonia found out, she panicked. She told Summer to never go through her belongings ever again. No other explanation. Just a somber retreat, then guilt: Sonia's *modus operandi*.

No, this doll wasn't a Marsalis prop.

Heart fluttering, Summer rode the vines into the water and located the string that had anchored the doll. Seaweed and vines grabbing at her legs and ankles, she played an imaginary game of tug of war, using the string to propel herself forward through the underwater thicket searching for its origin. When she got to the end she clawed through the mass of vines just under the surface, unraveling one ropey strand at a time, wishing she had a knife. Unable to see what her hands were doing, she picked and pulled vines until her fingers dug into something hard. Breathing hard and flushed with fear, she worked faster now, until she viewed a partially decomposed head.

Oh my God.

Panicking, Summer retreated, climbing up the bank and collapsing on a carpet of leaves, alternating between guttural sobs and dry heaves. It took her a while to regain enough composure to sit up. She looked around, listened to the birds whistling, the crickets chirping, the rustling sound made when a slight breeze tickled the trees. The way sunlight caught the lake was beautiful, she thought. Then she felt like something wasn't quite right, an object out of place; her intuition playing tricks? No. There, propped between two partially secreted tree branches, an unnatural object. Summer peered into the lens and realized Marsalis had watched the whole thing. Before she knew what she was doing, she'd ripped Marsalis's surveillance gear down and onto the ground, trampling it with her shoes. Then she flung it into the woods. Immediately after she was sorry; she had just giving Marsalis even more of a thrill.

A few minutes later, while Summer wound down the hiking trail, watching the sun shimmer on the lake, she tried to piece together what had happened. Sonia, her body and mind ravaged by melanoma, must have decided to return to the scene of her crime of abandonment. Summer always wondered why Sonia had accepted so much responsibility for Wib's lonely death. She believed she had killed them both with her inattentiveness, which would partially explain why she had doted so much on Summer, suffocating her for the better part of her childhood.

When Summer got to the lodge, she phoned the medical examiner.

Chantelle bitched about the extra work. "Two bodies in one day? What the hell kind of investigation are you conducting?"

"A very stressful one," Summer said.

"Do you at least have any idea who the victim is?"

Summer was shivering, her lips purple. Eventually she managed to say, "My mother."

CHAPTER 17

MELBA IGNACIO SAT BEHIND the smudged glass partition thumbing through a Bible. *They all find God in the slammer,* Summer thought, *like a jury would forgive them so long as they've let the Lord into their life.* Ignacio was on the road to 40, and a rough ride it had been. Acne scars ate at her cheeks. Gray roots poked through short black hair. A jaundiced dot marked her eye.

The phone pinned between her shoulder and ear, Summer held the note Rosie had passed her up to the glass. "This yours?"

Ignacio picked up the phone and said in a smoky voice, "You SK's lawyer?"

"That's right," Summer said.

"I got information about Gundy," Ignacio said. "You help me, I help you."

"You already have an attorney."

"Fuck, yeah, I know. Rosie and me, we go way the fuck

back. Grew up together. Same shitty neighborhood. But she won't help me out."

"If you asked her to spring you, she can't."

"I'm innocent, all right? I may be a cocksucker, but I ain't no dope shagger."

Summer held up the police report and tapped it with her finger. "You ran away from a cop and dropped ten vials of crack at her feet."

"Personal consumption, and I only had *two* vials," Ignacio explained. "They trumped up them charges and shit. I was framed."

"Why would the cops do that?"

"Look. Me and Gundy? We had this arrangement. He'd call, I'd come by. For two fucking years. I came by the night someone fucked him up good."

"What time?"

"He told me be there by ten but I was late, like twenty minutes. Had to find a sitter for my kid, 'cause my man and me had a fight."

"What does Gundy's place look like?"

"It's in the Prairie View district. Split-level action. Condo, sidewalk out front. The outside's painted this ugly baby diarrhea color."

Summer's mouth went dry. "Could you describe the person you saw?"

"That's why I got you here."

"Well?"

Ignacio regarded her cuticles. "All I'm gonna say now is that it wasn't no SK."

"How do you know?"

"We're in the same cellblock. See her every fucking day.

She's cool. Knows this kung fu shit, so the guards are afraid of her. Sometimes the motherfuckers beat the shit out of us for no reason. But they don't wanna fuck with here. She's chilled out the tensions between the *Cholos* and other Latinas, blacks, whites—like one happy fucking United Nations."

"You're telling me you saw someone leave Gundy's around the time of the murder. You get a good look?"

"Pretty good."

"What was she wearing?"

"I didn't say 'she'."

"He?"

"Didn't say 'he' neither."

"What *are* you saying?" Summer asked impatiently.

Ignacio folded her arms. "That'll cost you."

"Money? What are you going to do with that?"

"I ain't asking for money. I just want you to get me out of here."

Summer ground her molars. "Tell me about your relationship to Gundy. Were you lovers?"

"No lovin', just sex. He was into hardcore S&M, liked to hurt girls, drip candle wax, smack them around, tie them up. He ran a tab with Sexcorts, the place I worked. Most of the other girls wouldn't have nothing to do with him. I mean cra-a-azy. But, I ain't stupid. I don't have the look men want to know better anymore. I took what I could get, and what I could get was Gundy."

"There's not much I can do for you. This is a felony. The best you could do is cop a plea, maybe get it reduced from intent to sell to misdemeanor possession, although the D.A's reluctant to do that these days. With your record, no matter what, you're still going to do time."

"Bullshit. You know if you wanna get me out, you can. All you gotta do is talk to the *man*. Street-speak. Say for $1500, he'll lose your file for you. Then they gotta let you go. But you got to hurry. The trial starts tomorrow."

"You're asking a lot."

Ignacio shrugged. "Fifteen hundred bucks and a phone call's all I'm asking. But believe me, it's worth it."

Summer took a moment to think. It was risky. After Cruz, could she afford to bend the law again? Could this blow her case wide open? Or just blow it up? "I'm not promising anything," she said, "but say there's this miracle, and you get out. Will you testify under oath? Tell a jury you saw someone other than SK come out of his condo? Tell the court about Gundy's sexual perversions?"

"I'll do anything to get out of here. I want to see my baby. Can you understand that? I know I fucked up, but I gotta be there for him. I'm all he's got."

"Don't talk to the press, no newspapers, TV, nothing."

"I won't. Here's what you do. Talk to this lawyer, Eddie Brockton. He be the man that can make files disappear."

CHAPTER 18

HER ALARM WENT OFF AT 3:20, but Summer was already up, sipping peppermint tea to settle her jangly stomach.

She tuned into cable-access Channel 67, a local station with a hodgepodge of programs covered by the First Amendment. The original intention had been to foster community programs; instead, viewers were confronted with 24 hours of political diatribes, endless loops advertising escort services and phone sex, psychic babble, anarchist manifestos, and political extremism.

Summer endured the one-minute program break, and then the screen shifted into grainy video. She could see Jimi Cruz on the floor, his back propped against a dirty stone wall. He was tying his arm with a hose, one end stuck in his mouth. He was all attention as he held a lighter under a tablespoon. When powder bubbled into liquid, Cruz sucked it up with a syringe.

"It's good stuff?" Cruz asked.

"The best." Marsalis's voice, off camera. "And more where that came from."

Cruz smiled dreamily. He found a vein, and Summer watched the needle disappear into his arm, watched the plunger push the narc into him.

"Why did you come back to Haze County?" Marsalis asked. "Why didn't you stay in Las Vegas?"

Cruz's breathing was relaxed. He talked softly. "I didn't know anybody in Vegas, didn't know the scene there."

"That is not the reason, is it?"

"C'mon, man."

"You shouldn't have come back."

"I just met you. How do you know this?"

"Tell me the truth, Jimi, or I'm taking my heroin."

"Wait!" Cruz's eyes were sugar-glazed. "OK, OK. There was this lawyer, really cool. Beautiful girl. I was curious. I wondered, like, what's her deal? How could someone so pretty, so together, be so sad, you know? I just want to take care of her. Like by helping her, I'd be turning my own life around. Kick this habit, get a life. Stupid, huh?"

"Pointless," Marsalis said.

Cruz wretched, grasped his sternum with his hands. "That's a weird kick."

"It's the poison," Marsalis said. "You'll feel differently in a moment."

Cruz rolled onto his side. "Where'd you pick up that little bit of slang? I thought me and my friends were the only ones calling it that."

The camera panned closer. Pebbles of sweat swept over Cruz's face.

"By coming back, you have jeopardized the very person

you wanted to save," Marsalis said. "If the D.A. finds out, they will hold her responsible. This I cannot allow."

Cruz was almost unconscious. "You're not running me out of town, man."

"What is the last thing you wish to say, Jimi?"

"Huh?" More a groan than a question.

"You're going to die now," Marsalis said. "Tell me the very last thought you'll ever have."

Cruz was able to whisper one last word before his head flopped against the floor and his eyes rolled heavenward: "*Summer.*"

CHAPTER 19

A
LL SUMMER COULD THINK ABOUT, while a maid led her along the outer edge of Brockton's stucco house and to his swimming pool, was death: Sonia's death, Wib's death, Cruz's death, Gundy's death. She barely felt alive herself, as if each passing took a piece of her with it.

The maid left Summer with Brockton, who was nestled under an umbrella with a 6-foot redhead. Other B-girl clients sunbathed topless.

Brockton talked from behind sunglasses. "I was beginning to think you didn't like me."

"I don't." Summer addressed the redhead. "Could you excuse us?"

The woman threw Summer a catty look. Summer returned it.

Brockton mediated. "Beat it, Ramona, *por favor.*"

Ramona took her time unwinding from Brockton. Before sashaying away, she branded him with a kiss.

Summer said, "I'm amazed how boob jobs have changed

America's landscape."

Brockton rubbed oil on his nipples. "Don't tell me your tits are real."

Summer spun her eyes in disgust.

"I insulted you?" Brockton said. "Let me make it up to you."

"That's not why I'm here."

"It's on the house."

"All right."

"Did you know that The Latin Brothers had a contract out on Gundy?"

Summer had been so wrapped up with Strickland it hadn't occurred to her that others could be to blame for Gundy's death. But she couldn't let Brockton know this. "I've heard things."

Brockton laughed skeptically. "For a high class broad, you're a lousy liar. See my girls over there, soaking up my sun, drinking my booze, snorting my coke, using me for my money? They have three things on their minds: getting high, living the good life, and staying out of jail. I tell you, whores live a lot more honest than you."

"I never thought of you as someone interested in truth."

"When are you going to leave that dead-end P.D. job and make some real money? Best thing that ever happened to me was getting bounced from the D.A.'s office. I mean, look around, Sugar: five-bedroom home, three bathrooms, Jacuzzi, swimming pool, hot and cold running babes. Money talks, bullshit walks."

"Did your phone sex operator teach you that or did you pick it up on your own?"

Brockton guffawed, patted his chest. "Have a seat."

"I'll stand, thanks," Summer said. "I want you to consider

this conversation covered under attorney-client privilege."

Brockton removed his shades and arched his eyebrows. "You want to hire *me*?"

"As a matter of fact, yes."

"And all this time I've been trying to hire you and you've been dissing me over it. Oh, well, the enemy of my enemy is my friend. I thought Hightower let you off the hook on that aiding and abetting deal."

"This is different. Want the job?"

"I'll have one of my in-house whores draw up the contracts."

"Do I take that as a 'yes'?"

"Want a snort to seal the deal?" He placed the sunglasses on the deck and offered Summer a mirror, a hash mark of coke on it.

Summer pushed the mirror back at him. "I know someone who was framed on a drug deal. She's not even my client. What would it take to get her out of jail?"

"She charged with just possession, or possession with intent to sell?"

"Both."

"She have priors?"

"Prostitution, but no drugs."

"Why do you care?"

"Let's just say I care."

Brockton eyed her. "Bullshit. If I'm going to get your playmate out of the pen I need to know everything."

"That's not what I heard. You still have all your contacts with the D.A. For you, it's one phone call."

"What do I get out of it?"

"What's the usual fee?"

Brockton spread his arms out, indicated the pool, home, and whores. "Do I look like I need your money?"

"What *do* you want?"

He leaned over the mirror and, his eyes trained on Summer's chest, and sucked up a line. He wiped his nose. "I want you, baby."

"No, seriously."

"I am serious."

"I heard it's a simple cash transaction."

"Usually it is, but since you've been ignoring me all these years after our night of margarita magic, I've decided I don't want your money. I want you."

"I don't think the ABA recognizes that as a legitimate form of billing," Summer said.

Brockton sniffled. "They don't recognize making files disappear either."

"I'm not having sex with you, Brockton."

"Then no deal."

After slamming Brockton's backyard gate shut, Summer hopped into her truck. Why had she come? Was her case *that* weak? Maybe Raines was right. Maybe the way she was going, the law would snap back.

On her desk at the office, Chantelle's report on Strickland was waiting for her. Summer ripped it open and skimmed through the scientific jargon until she got to the point: Strickland and the DNA from the letter did not match. So he hadn't died in that car wreck.

Summer held her breath. Could she use this to raise enough doubt in a jury's eyes to get SK acquitted? She curled up in her chair and sat Indian style.

Chantelle had included a handwritten note:

Dear Summer,

Be very careful. If Strickland is alive and finds out you are looking for him, you could be in danger. Serial killers who have been underground a long time do not like to be rousted.

I am very sorry about your mother. Let me know if there is anything I can do.

Chantelle.

The image of Sonia being excavated from Fayres Lake haunted Summer: Chantelle standing beside her, draping a blanket over her shoulders. It had taken three divers to lift Sonia's corpse out of the water. Sonia had wrapped chains around cinder blocks to anchor her to the bottom. Clearly a suicide, Chantelle had told Summer.

Sonia had returned to the source of her guilt and died alongside the memory of her long-lost child. And now Summer wasn't sure if Sonia and Wib were even her parents. She trusted nothing Marsalis said. But without his help, she might never find out the truth.

Summer seeped into her chair. She hadn't eaten or slept since finding Sonia's body. Her clothes were a half-size too large now, hanging loosely. She checked her face in a compact mirror, bemoaning the paleness of her cheeks, the boniness of her collarbone. The bags under her eyes were so big they couldn't be stowed in the overhead compartment of a plane. She was going to have to take better care of herself.

But first, her voice mail, a reel of messages. The crematorium said to pick up Sonia's ashes. Mahakavi wanted to know when he could expect Strickland's letter back. Chantelle asked how Summer was feeling. And Tai called: important, he said.

She dialed his cell phone.

"Hey," Tai said. "I'm up in Strickland land, a real logger's town. Been putting a lot of miles in for you, which I hope you appreciate."

"What have you got for me?" she asked.

"You're going love this. I'm 100 percent certain Marsalis and Strickland are not the same psycho. I'll spare you the details, but suffice to say there's a lot of twisted shit in both their lives. I have one more thing to check on. If it pans out, you're definitely going to want to buy me dinner."

"It would have to be one unbelievable chunk of information," she said.

"Does that mean yes?"

"Bye." She hung up. When Tai got back to Haze County, she would get him out of her hair by siccing him on Strickland, see what he could turn up.

She went downstairs and bought a slice of pizza, and then went to the conference room. Rosie was there, listening to her iPod while sipping soup. Summer fished the pizza out of the bag, held it over the trash, and dripped grease.

The only sound in the room was emanating from Rosie's earphones. Rosie shut off the music.

Uncomfortable silence. Finally, Rosie tried to reach out. "You ever meet with Ignacio?"

"Yes," Summer said.

"What did she want?"

"She claims she saw a woman, and not SK, flee Gundy's place at the time of the murder. But she wouldn't talk unless I sprung her."

Rosie's mouth dropped open. "Oh, fuck, you are in luck. The judge had to throw the case out."

"*What?*"

"Yeah. They couldn't find her file. As a last resort, the D.A. offered to plead it down to a misdemeanor, but I held out. Glad I did because she walked."

Summer pitched the pizza slice on the table. She tried to run through all of the possibilities, but couldn't figure out who, besides Brockton—and he didn't even know who Ignacio was—could have helped her gain her freedom.

"Who was the prosecutor?" she asked.

Rosie grinned. "Raines. And boy was he pissed."

Summer paced the room. "I have to find Ignacio. Without her testimony, SK is history."

"You want to know where to look?"

"No."

Rosie poked herself in the chest. "You want *me* to find her?"

"Please."

Rosie didn't say anything. Summer could tell she was being pulled in two different directions.

Summer sat on the edge of the table. "I need you, Rosie."

Rosie gazed at the ceiling, shaking her head and talking all professorially. "I can't do it. Sorry. SK is your problem. I've got a lot of my own shit to do, and I can't be spending days tracking down a witness for you."

She wrapped up her headphone wires and Summer watched her slip out of the room, wondering what had caused their friendship to fizzle.

Summer wondered if she should get Tai in on this, but was afraid he would find out that she had tried to hire Brockton to interfere. She took a nervous bite of pizza. It was cold, so she chucked it in the trash. She swept into her office to call Brockton.

"So," he said smoothly, "you change your mind after all? Well, the price just went up. I can just taste your—"

Summer dropped the phone. If Brockton hadn't sprung Ignacio, who had?

CHAPTER 20

TO ACCOMMODATE PUBLIC INTEREST and the press, Judge Hightower had moved the trial to a courtroom that was spacious but a monument to budget-cutting dreariness. Pew-like sections were rimmed by strips of Chianti-colored carpeting marked with threadbare patches. Morning light streamed through the windows and around faux-Roman columns, cutting the court into jagged parts. Art deco light fixtures had been pulled out and replaced by fluorescent rods, some of which were blinking or sizzling or dead. Journalists were relegated to the back of the court, along with other sensation-seekers, while Hightower's crusty bailiffs, Ed Sprague and Gus Patterson, flanked the judge on both sides.

SK sat at the defense table in her jail jumpsuit while Summer eyed the jury pool, six dozen Haze County folks slouched in chairs and benches who would determine SK's fate. Summer was careful not to touch eyes with anyone. She didn't want anyone to know she was mentally taking notes, tallying the number of Blacks, Asians, Latinos, ex-hippies, and Nancy Pelosi liberals—anyone who stood out in the predominantly starchy white crowd.

It was no secret that both the defense and prosecution played the race game, trying to pack juries with folks predisposed to aid their cases. If the defendant was a Black or Hispanic male (about 90 percent of the time in Haze County) the prosecution, as a rule, would strike anyone who worked with the poor—teachers, social workers—and also people of the same race, especially older women who, because they might view the defendant like a grandson, would be reluctant to vote guilty. Since SK wasn't male, Black or Hispanic, Summer figured Raines's jury selection strategy would be to strike as many women, minorities, and college graduates as possible.

The defense was little better when it came to race. Summer planned to keep unassimilated Asians off the jury because they'd emigrated from authoritarian states and tended to defer to authority; Republicans (she didn't like Republicans); upper-middle class Hispanics, who were often conservative; gun owners; religious zealots; and anyone related to a cop.

In Haze County, that was just about everyone.

Which was why Summer viewed the law as a subjective interpretation of the truth. Justice didn't exist in any penal code handbook, but in the hearts and heads of the police, prosecutors, and ultimately, the jury. And verdicts hinged, in large part, on how well lawyers played the jury selection game and venue: acquittals were as dependent on where the defendant committed the crime as on the skills of the attorneys—sometimes more.

As in real estate, the three most important elements in a criminal case were location, location, location.

Summer glanced at Raines, who while posing for the Haze County Register sketch artist—cameras were barred—was also tabulating the odds.

But it was Summer who was playing the long shot. The evidence and the whole Haze County judicial system were stacked against her. Plus, her client was barely speaking to her. In fact, Summer wasn't sure why SK had retained her.

Summer turned to SK and spoke in a low murmur. "It's not too late to ditch the prison garb. A jury would find it a lot easier to believe you're innocent if you would dress innocent. A dress, a little makeup."

"I told you," SK said. "I'm not playing this game. If I'm going down, I'm going down on my own terms. Maybe the cops will succeed in framing me, but at least I'll be able to live with myself."

Summer made sure no one was listening, and then in a hissy whisper said, "This is a capital case. If you don't start doing what I tell you, it's not going to be a question of you living with yourself. It'll be a question of you dying alone."

SK offered Summer a mock laugh. "You don't engender much confidence. You've won one case."

"The last two times I went down to the jail, you refused to see me."

"I had nothing to say to you."

"Then why keep me? Why not file a Marsden?"

SK looked at the ceiling and sighed. "We share something in common."

Summer stared at her client's profile: the thick red ringlets brushing her ears, her deep green eyes, the freckles raindropped onto worn cheeks, and sensed the tremor of tension beneath her client's composure. SK was expending enormous energy just keeping herself together.

Summer's eyes stung. "Yes, we do. But you're running out of time. If you don't want to try and save yourself for you, do it for the women like us. What will happen to them if you're convicted without your even putting up a legitimate legal challenge? What kind of impact will your life, and your work, have then?"

SK shot Summer a bitter look.

Hightower gave the word, and Sprague shepherded twelve prospectives into the jury box, where they awaited his queries. The judge sat regal but pale. Summer had seen him on TV at a fundraiser for cystic fibrosis the night before, pumping hands, slapping backs, pandering for votes; the race against Raines for the bench was close. Hightower wasted no opportunity to get out on the campaign trail.

He spoke into a microphone. "Testing, test—" There was squeaky feedback until Sprague adjusted the controls. "Can you all hear me? Good. We are gathered here today to bring this man and woman together in holy matrimony."

He was greeted by shocked silence. Then he smiled and said, "Gotcha."

The jury pool and members of the press broke into laughter. Summer sat in silence. She had heard Hightower's shtick before.

"Thank you for attending," he said. "We'll be questioning you in groups of twelve. The rest of you, please remain silent." He turned to the twelve people in the jury box and asked, "Do any of you feel that you cannot render an impartial verdict in this case?"

A smattering of hands went up. Some judges would automatically have excluded them, but Hightower rarely exempted panelists: his view was that as a judge he had a responsibility to make sure that no one should be able to skip out from their civic duty. But the real reason was that since Haze County was Law and Order U.S.A., and any pool of jurors was bound to share these sentiments, the fewer exemptions he offered meant the more exemptions the defense wasted. Since many trials were won or lost at jury selection, this contributed to Hightower's high conviction rate.

The judge consulted a seating chart. "Mr. Andrews?"

A man with a 30-something face, a 40-something body, and bone-white 50-something hair stood, struggling to pull his jeans over his belly.

Hightower told him to sit, then asked, "What is it that could prevent you from judging this case fairly?"

Andrews absently fingered a pack of cigarettes straining against his shirt pocket. "My brother's a policeman. I know they don't arrest somebody less they know they got the right guy."

"But is there any reason you couldn't weigh the evidence, give the defendant a fair trial? Remember: In our country, someone is innocent until proven guilty."

"That's the law all right," Andrews said, "but I think if the police arrest you, you're guilty. I'm a taxpayer. I think the guy on trial should prove their innocence."

"Ah, the Napoleonic code." Hightower forced a smile. Even now, Summer realized, he was campaigning. "Unfortunately, Mr. Andrews, our law states otherwise. Let me ask you again. Could you be fair and impartial, follow the rules that have been set forth?"

"I got a business. I'm a private contractor. I don't work, I don't eat."

The judge scratched an ear and waited.

Andrews, wheezing like steamed heat, shifted in his chair, finally saying, "Yeah, I could be fair, impartial, follow the laws, whatever."

The judge massaged his knuckles. "I'm glad to hear it, Mr. Andrews," he said, and moved on to the next prospective juror.

Summer, working from a grid, made a note to strike Andrews. She only had ten such challenges, ten opportunities to shape the jury.

SK tugged on Summer's sleeve. "When do we get to question them?"

Summer leaned close, gently placing her hand on SK's shoulder, not only to keep their conversation private but to show the assembled that there was nothing to fear. "During *voir dire*, judges have the option to question jurors themselves or let the lawyers do it," Summer whispered. "Judge Hightower likes to keep a tight lid on things, so he questions the jury pool. It certainly speeds up jury selection. We may be able to get through it in one long day. And it could work to our advantage."

"How?"

"The legislature gave judges this power because too many defense attorneys were trying their cases before the jury pools. It was intended as a sop to the prosecution, but it often works to the advantage of the defense. Judges aren't as good at weeding out the artichokes, the assorted nuts and crazies who, if not carefully questioned, can turn twelve-oh into eleven-one."

"You're going for a hung jury?"

Summer tapped her fingers on her state law handbook. "I'm going for anything I can get."

Hightower held up his seating chart to the light. "Mrs. Rye... Rah-Gee—"

Summer keyed in on a tangy twang from the back row. "It's pronounced *Rah-shay*, but spelled R-a-s-i-e-j," a busty, polyester-clad woman said. Her hair was bleached and teased; on her lips, she wore talc-white lipstick. Second-generation trailer-park trash, Summer thought. She could almost smell the hair spray.

"Excuse me, Ms. Rasiej," Judge Hightower said.

"Mrs.," she corrected.

"Excuse me, *Mrs.* Rasiej. Do you feel you can't be objective?"

"That's what I'm saying, Your Honor. I have a lot of trouble with those kinds of people."

Hightower rubbed his chin thoughtfully . "Do you personally know Ms. Killington?"

"Only from the TV."

"I see. Well, this is as good a time as any to tell you all that you are ordered to ignore anything you've seen or heard through the media. Now, what kind of people are you referring to?"

"My husband says she's a—a lesbian," Rasiej articulated with distaste. "That goes against the word of God."

There were some hisses from the visitors' gallery. Hightower immediately made use of his gavel. "Quiet back there or I'll clear the court of spectators."

When he had commanded full attention, he grunted, "Uh-huh, uh-huh, but Mrs. Rasiej, if Ms. Killington is a lesbian, and I'm not saying she is, but if she were, it wouldn't matter one whit in my courtroom. We are gathered here to determine whether Ms. Killington is guilty of breaking our laws, not God's law."

"It's all one and the same to me," Rasiej said.

Ignoring Raines's sniggling grin, Summer stood and addressed the court. "Your Honor, I request a sidebar."

"Request denied, Ms. Neuwirth."

Summer settled back into her chair. She could feel SK's rage over not being able to set the record—or her sexual preference—straight. She put her hand around SK's shoulder, but realizing the message it was sending, quickly removed it. She could hear a man next to Rasiej hiss, "She ain't no lez-bean. She was married."

Rasiej talked back. "Is that so?"

Summer thought, *Yeah, to an abortion doctor. So long, Rasiej.* She crossed her off her list.

Hightower worked his gavel. "That is quite enough of this. Do not talk unless—"

He was interrupted by a demonstration. A half-dozen women stood, holding placards—"Free SK from the Fatherland" and "No Justice, No Peace" were two that stuck in Summer's mind—and chanted, "Fuck the system! Fuck the system!" Summer wondered how they had been able to sneak them into court undetected.

Hightower shouted, "If you do not cease this moment, I will hold you in contempt of court!"

Summer detected the shadow of a grin crossing SK's face. "Did you know about this?" she asked over the din.

SK's eyes were luminescent, but she didn't say anything.

Hightower exploded. "Bailiffs! Get them out of here *now!*"

When Sprague and Patterson moved down the aisle to round up the protesters, the women, obviously expert in the techniques of civil disobedience, went limp and crumpled to the ground, continuing their chant. Unable to handle more than one at a time, Sprague had to call for backup.

Summer was fuming. "Don't you see what damage this is doing to our case? You've done more to turn the jury pool against you than a hundred tabloid stories."

"They're going to convict me anyway," SK said matter-of-factly.

"If you're so sure of that, then why not plead guilty now and get it over with? Why put yourself through a trial?"

SK didn't say anything. The protestors continued their cries. Everybody seemed to be talking at once.

Aware that all attention was on the disturbance, Summer grabbed SK's wrist. SK responded by bending Summer's thumb back, but stopped when Summer said, "You're a coward, Stephanie Killington. If you want to die a martyr, then fine, you win. We'll get you another attorney. But that will be your only victory."

Summer let go of SK and snatched her State Penal Code handbook from the table. She threw it into her briefcase and got up to leave. "I don't need this bullshit. I've represented glue sniffers with more sense than you."

SK grabbed Summer's arm and pulled her down in her chair. "I'm sorry. I shouldn't have let this happen without telling you first."

"You shouldn't have let this happen period," Summer said. "You've already shot yourself in the foot with this jury pool. Are you scared to fight them in court? Do you think you can win with pyrotechnics like this? It may give you satisfaction, but it's the fastest way to end up on death row."

SK shut her eyes and bit her bottom lip. "You're right," she said after a moment of reflection. "But show me something, Summer. Show me we can win. Give me something to hang my hopes on. Anything. If you can do that, I'll do whatever you say."

Summer was still reeling with anger. She heard herself heaving breaths. "If you ever pull anything like this again, I'll drop you so hard you'll hit escape velocity without even leaving your cell."

More bailiffs busted in. It took five minutes to clear the protestors out. When order had been restored, the tension in the room was so tight you could strum it. Hightower, eyes and face scarlet, looked out on the remaining spectators and said with uncontained aggravation, "If any of you even so much as yawn in my court, I will bar all visitors."

Summer stood. "Your Honor. May I approach the bench?"

Hightower shook his head. "Not if you're going to ask the court to provide a new jury pool. I am not going to send these people home just because some hecklers tried to infect my court with their agenda."

Although she knew there was no chance of changing his mind, Summer offered Hightower an incredulous smile. "But Your Honor—"

"That will be all, Ms. Neuwirth. Now, Mrs. Rasiej. I believe we were discussing the issue of fairness."

"Yes, sir," Rasiej said. "And now that I know the score, I think I can be fair."

"Splendid, Ms. Rasiej," Hightower said with plastic courtliness.

Even without looking Summer could see Raines's dreamy smile. Fifteen minutes into jury selection, protestors had sabotaged SK's case, and already Summer would be forced to waste two peremptory challenges.

It was a grueling process. By the time court broke for lunch, Summer had gone through four more, striking a woman with a thick Cantonese accent she was sure would have trouble processing testimony, a man in the National Guard, a retired minister, and a skinhead. Raines used up four of his exemptions on the few minorities the judge had questioned—two Hispanic women and two of the five Blacks present.

In the afternoon, after Raines had dismissed his third black prospective juror, Summer set her strategy in motion. "Your Honor," she said, "I request the court be cleared."

Hightower nodded. He checked his watch. "I think it's time the jury pool got a break. Take fifteen minutes to get a cup of coffee, relax. We'll call you when we need you."

When the court was empty, save for the judge and bailiffs, Summer, SK, Raines, the press, and some spectators, Summer addressed the court. "I have no choice but to motion for a Wheeler objection, Your Honor. Mr. Raines has struck three of only five African-Americans. It's clear he's basing these objections on the basis of their race."

For a change, Raines was calm. Which meant he was confident, almost cocky, Summer thought. "Preposterous," he said matter-of-factly. "I struck the first man, Mr. Starks, because he said he'd a bad experience with the police. And I excluded the second, Ms. Griffey, because she didn't give me the impression that she was paying attention. And the third, Mr. Roberts, why, he wouldn't make eye contact with me. And I never sit someone on a jury who won't make eye contact with me."

Hightower scratched his chin. "On the surface, there does seem to be *prima facie* evidence of bias on the part of the prosecutor. I'm going to take a few minutes to sort through this."

There went Raines's composure. He protested, "I can't believe you can't see that this is a ploy by the defense to—"

The judge cut him off abruptly and angrily. "Are you telling me, Mr. Raines, that as a judge, I should *not* take a moment to reflect without your less than sage input?"

Raines wouldn't quit. "I have never been accused of—"

"Be quiet, Raines, or I'll hold you in contempt. What do you say to that?"

"Your Honor—"

"Quiet!" Hightower yelled, before escaping into chambers.

Summer could see that their veneer of civility had been stripped away by Raines's political ambitions. She delighted herself with a plan to anonymously send one of Raines's flyers to Hightower, the one that a volunteer had been handing out in front of the courthouse. It read: *Say No to Plea Bargains and Soft Sentencing. Say Yes to Seymour Raines.* Then she thought better of it: Why give Hightower any more incentive to hang her client?

Minutes later the judge was back. "I did a little research," he said. "In the case of *Taylor vs. Madison*, hostile body language on the part of a juror can be used as a rationale for removal. So I'm going to deny the motion."

Summer had expected this. She knew Hightower wouldn't change his whole judicial philosophy just to wage war on Raines. But it was valuable leverage nevertheless. She rose. "Your Honor, I want my objection entered into the record. Why would Mr. Roberts make eye contact with Mr. Raines? *You* were addressing him, not the prosecution. If Mr. Raines were on the prowl at a singles bar, I could see why eye contact would be important. But not in this instance."

There were snickers from the press.

Raines jiggled his foot. "Your Honor, that was uncalled for. I ask the court to inform counselor—"

Hightower pounded his gavel. "Order, order. That's quite enough, Ms. Neuwirth. Your objection is noted, but my decision stands." To Sprague, he said, "Bring the prospective jurors in."

The questioning continued. Summer hoarded the few peremptories she had left, passing a few jurors she wished she didn't have to—a male Hispanic hedge fund manager, a Christian housewife, a personal trainer with libertarian leanings. Raines excluded another low-income Hispanic and a social worker.

When Raines struck Didi Banks, the fourth of five African Americans in the pool, Summer jumped to her feet. "Objection, Your Honor. The prosecution—"

"Hold on, Ms. Neuwirth," Hightower said. He glared at Raines.

Raines shuffled his feet, but said nothing.

Tense silence was interrupted only by journalists scratching notes on pads or tapping on laptops.

Eventually, Hightower sighed. "Objection overruled."

"Can I go?" Banks asked. "Don't got no baby-sitter and school's out, Judge."

"You are excused," Hightower said, keeping taut eyes trained on Raines.

Banks picked up her belongings, and stumbling over shoes and ankles, made her way through the narrow aisle and out of the court. But it wasn't Banks Summer wanted. She had set her trap. She hoped Raines would fall for it.

The late afternoon sun yielded five o'clock shadows inside the court. Hightower asked the assembled to stay late to finish the process. Eleven jurors had been seated, with one slot left. Summer needed an advocate for SK on the jury; someone who, if the issue centered around reasonable doubt, would possess the ability to reason and lean toward acquittal as a matter of principle and law. If Summer were a high-priced private attorney, had the resources of someone like Eddie Brockton, she would have retained a private detective to perform background checks on each prospective juror.

Instead, she had to rely on intuition and experience. Her whole strategy rested precariously on one juror. If she could get her sworn in, then SK had a shot at a hung jury. (Summer didn't even fantasize about acquittal.) If she couldn't, then SK would have to start planning for the next life because this one would be over.

Hightower, his voice marred by fatigue, began questioning the last minority juror, ShaRon Robinson. She was heavy and carried it well, wearing a quiet beige suit that contrasted with her autumn-leaf skin. Her eyes were round and large, as if she were asking a question or surprised by the response. Neat, professional, Black—just the kind of juror Raines would strike.

The air in the courtroom was tight; Summer saw Bragg, the Haze County Register reporter, flip over a page in his notebook and continue scribbling.

"Ms. Robinson," the judge asked, "is the defendant innocent or guilty?"

Robinson took a moment to think. "All I know, Your Honor, is that the accused is innocent until proven otherwise. So logically, for now, I'd have to say she's innocent."

"Do you feel you can be fair and impartial?"

"Absolutely."

"Do you have a view of the police either way?"

Robinson sat with her hands clasped over her pocketbook. "I'm not a fan of gross generalizations. Some police are good and some are bad, just like everything else. That's what I've learned in my line of work: You have to deal with things on a case-by-case basis."

"What is this line of work?"

"I run a small software company. As you can imagine, it requires a keen eye for detail. If things don't add up, you have to go back and find the problem; otherwise you could lose out on an important contract."

"What happens if you can't locate the problem?"

"I don't know," she said. "I always find the glitches. Sometimes it takes a while, that's all. With a little elbow grease, anything is possible."

"Have you had any bad experiences with the police or know someone who has?"

Robinson didn't hesitate. "Yes."

The judge nodded. "I see. Would it pain you too much to tell me about it?"

She searched for the right words. "I once spent, um, two days in the county jail."

"What was the charge?"

"Jaywalking. But I wasn't guilty and the charges were dropped. I was downtown, Christmas shopping, and I had all these bags. I was tired and I wanted to get home. I guess I was standing one step off the curb when someone grabbed my arm. I pulled it away and a uniformed policeman told me I was under arrest. I couldn't believe it. When I protested the treatment I was receiving, the officer told me that just to teach me a lesson, he was going to put me through the judicial system."

"And..." Hightower's voice cracked. He cleared his throat. "And yet you say that you don't hold anti-police feelings?"

Robinson smiled. "I've also encountered good policemen. When my mother had a heart attack, a patrolman saved her life. There are all kinds of people in this world, and since I don't like being prejudged on the basis of my race or profession, I don't do it to others."

"What happened after you were released from County?"

"The charges were dropped. I lodged a complaint, but the officer wasn't even reprimanded."

"But if you are chosen to serve you could be fair?"

"Yes, sir, that's what I'm saying."

Hightower leaned back in his chair and swiveled, looking over to Summer. "Well, Ms. Neuwirth?"

Summer spoke to the whole courtroom, the press, the spectators, Raines and Hightower, and especially the seated jurors. This was no time to play it safe. "College-educated, impartial, a successful entrepreneur not afraid of hard work. How could anyone interested in justice not want someone like Ms. Robinson on a jury?"

She saw Raines trying not to squirm.

Normally, Hightower didn't go in for this kind of grandstanding, especially from defense attorneys, but Summer could see his anger over Raines's primary challenge was clouding his judgment. "I take it the defense intends to pass Ms. Robinson?" he said.

"Oh, yes, Your Honor. The defense believes Ms. Robinson would make a fine juror." She sat down, but couldn't resist adding, "Of course, I can't speak for Mr. Raines."

A few titters echoed from the back where the press pool sat.

"Order, order," Hightower said mechanically. "And the prosecution?"

All attention was on Raines. If he struck Robinson, the last minority, he was opening himself up to a possible mistrial, maybe even leaving the door open for the Court of Appeals to overturn the conviction. The press, which included reporters from all over the country, would savage him, portraying him and the whole Haze County judicial system as racist and unjust.

On the other hand, Robinson was exactly the kind of juror he didn't want. If she didn't end up jury foreman, she might end up a powerful player behind the scenes. Summer could feel Raines battle his indecision. His face was balled up tight, his crow's feet etched deeper. Finally, he said, "I'm forced to agree with my esteemed colleague. The prosecution accepts Ms. Robinson."

Summer softly clucked her tongue. *Bad move,* she thought.

SK, a grin stretching her face, flicked Summer's arm with the back of her hand. She didn't say anything; she didn't have to.

Hightower kept the pool intact until 6:45, until the last two alternates had been added to the panel. So it stood: The jury would be mostly white, with the Hispanic hedge fund manager and Robinson, and cut down the middle on gender: an electrician, secretary, computer magazine editor, caterer, church volunteer, a retired accountant, and the owner of a mail-order shoe company rounding out the jury. The two alternates were both gun-toting law-and-order types, but Summer had run out of peremptories and knew they probably wouldn't get to sit in on the decision anyway.

"All right, ladies and gentlemen," Hightower said. "For those who have been selected, we will meet back here at 8:45 tomorrow. For those of you who were not, please head over to Room Six. They will let you know where you should go next. Thank you. Court is adjourned."

CHAPTER 21

NEXT TO THE COURT WAS THE LOCKUP, a way station for defendants waiting transport back to jail. Patterson had already led SK inside to a solitary cell furnished with the standard issue concrete floor, slate bench, and a lonesome toilet.

Before Summer was allowed in, Sprague took possession of her briefcase, keys, pens—anything sharp or heavy. Then he began unlocking the ten-inch-thick door separating the lockup from the court.

"What a day," Sprague said, flipping through a dozen keys on a crammed key ring before he found the right one. "How come every time you appear in Judge Hightower's court, something fucked up happens? Hell, one of your client's hairy-legged dyke pals bit me on the arm." He turned the key in the lock and opened the door.

Summer followed him down a tight, detergent-scented hallway. Sprague's shoulders just missed brushing the walls by inches.

"She draw blood?" Summer asked.

Sprague showed her his wrist marked with a patch of sausage red. "Nah."

"That's probably because you don't have any."

He tossed her a coarse look, then ran his club along the bars of the cell. SK was inside, lying on a slate bench. "Your shyster has arrived, little lady," Sprague said. "And don't try anything, because I'll be watching from outside." He pointed with his club to a camera perched above. To Summer, he said, "Transport's coming in twenty minutes."

He left, the slamming of the metal door behind him punctuating the silence. This was the first time Summer had been alone with SK without a barrier of glass between them since her arraignment. Summer stood on one side of the iron bars; SK slid off the bench and stood on the other. Their faces were just inches apart.

Summer said, "We're on the same side, right? We have to work together. Otherwise, we won't win."

"I got the message," SK said. "No more protests. I'll wear whatever clothes you want. I'll do what ever you want me to. I just want you to guarantee I'll get a chance to tell my side."

Summer sidestepped SK's request. "Your side? What *is* your side?"

"That I was framed."

"Why?"

SK backed away and stood with her arms crossed over her chest. "Maybe because the cops are a bunch of fascist pigs. I don't know."

"Bashing cops may make you feel good, but it never plays well with a jury, unless it's packed with people from a community that's been victimized by them. If this were L.A., sure, we'd have a shot with that kind of strategy. If this were New York

City or Chicago, ditto. But this is lily-white Haze County, U.S.A. Did you see many folks today other than ShaRon Robinson who didn't fit that description?"

"It's not fair," SK said.

"It's reality." Summer ran her hand up one of the bars and squeezed. It was steely cold. She took it off and put it against her forehead to cool her fever. "Look, Officer Tyler may not be a bastion of competence, but I checked his personnel records, and in the fifteen years he's been on the force no one's ever complained about him planting evidence. We would have to show a motive or a predisposition on his part to alter evidence."

"He hates me and what I do. Isn't that motive enough?"

"How do you know he hates you?"

"Because of the way he treated me when my husband was killed. He—"

SK's revelation jolted Summer. She shook the bars. "Are you saying Tyler was the investigating officer in Jonathan Sadbury's homicide?"

"Yes. And he made his views about Jonathan's work quite clear."

Summer mentally flogged herself. How could she have missed this connection? "What did he say?"

"I overheard him telling another cop that the murder of an abortion doctor was just God's way of evening the score. That's not admissible, is it?"

It was if SK took the stand and testified, which Summer wasn't going to allow. She plowed on. "Do you remember who he told this to?"

"No."

"Let me think about this for a bit. In the meantime, I'm going to have to scrounge around for some clothes for you.

What's your size?"

"Six. Listen, it's not easy for me having to rely on someone. Until I met Jonathan, I did everything on my own, because experience showed me I couldn't trust anyone. But you showed something today. I really appreciate everything you've done, and I want to give back something to you."

"Wait until after the trial to thank me. We may have lucked out a little with the jury, but the judge has a very narrow view of what evidence is admissible, a view that substantially favors the prosecution. Plus the evidence *is* pretty damning. I don't want you getting your hopes up."

"Believe me, my hopes are not up. But I still think I have something I can give you."

"Oh?"

SK reached through the bars. Her hand grazed Summer, who leaned out of harm's way.

SK grabbed the bars with both hands and peered through. "I can help you with your fear."

"I'd better go," Summer said, starting for the door.

"I feel your fear, Summer," SK called. "And it's not just because you were raped. It's something else, something from your past, something you've been afraid to face up to."

Summer stopped a few paces away.

"There are two dynamics here," SK explained. "First of all, when that man raped you, he took away your feeling of security, and you've been running scared since. Every loud noise, every time you walk alone, even when you're in your home behind locked doors, you don't feel safe. That's a terrible burden to carry. Fortunately, it's easy to fix. The other dynamic, your past, I can show you the way—but you'll have to take the journey alone."

Summer checked her wrist for the time but realized Sprague

had her watch. "I don't have a lot of time now."

SK rolled up the sleeves of her prison jumpsuit. "Of course. You don't trust easily. I've seen it more times than you know. But come here."

Summer approached cautiously. She stopped a foot from the cage.

"Most assaults against women occur when a man grabs her from behind," SK said. "Is that what happened to you?"

Summer's mouth was cotton-dry. She tried to swallow. "Yes."

"What you want to do is master a couple of basic moves to protect yourself. No matter how strong a man is, he has soft spots." SK turned her back on Summer and leaned into the bars. "Grab me like you were grabbed."

Summer reached between the bars and tentatively held the side of her hand against SK's throat. "He had a knife."

"It doesn't matter. Push your hand into my neck harder."

Summer did. SK twisted Summer's pinky with one hand, pulling the imaginary knife away from her body while at the same time throwing a lightning-fast elbow between the bars, stopping millimeters from her eye.

SK released her. "Now, you try it," she said.

They reversed positions. When Summer felt SK's hand around her neck, she grabbed at it but couldn't get a grip. SK tightened the hold and Summer couldn't breathe. Rasping, she said, "Stop," but nothing came out. She panicked, flailing away, trying to get at SK's hair, but she couldn't. She was feeling weak, about to pass out.

When Sprague unbolted the lock from outside, SK let go. Summer fell forward, holding her neck and breathing like a hummingbird.

"Never panic," SK said, "and be sure that you focus all your power on one point: the pinky."

"What the hell is wrong with you?" Summer coughed.

She could hear Sprague loping down the hallway, his keys jangling. Summer held up her hand like a stop sign. "It's OK. She was just demonstrating something."

Sprague eyed them coldly. "I don't like the look of this. You're going to have to leave, and I'm throwing this psycho in irons."

"I said everything is OK. You are not in a position to judge what is appropriate behavior between a lawyer and a client. Now, leave us alone. We still have some time left."

Sprague checked his watch. "Ten more minutes. Then she goes back to the pokey."

After Sprague left SK wrapped her hair into a knot. "Let's try it again, keeping in mind what I said."

This time, Summer was able to slide her hand between SK's pinky and her neck and torque SK's finger. When she peeled the hand away, she threw the point of her elbow behind her, in the direction of SK's face, but struck solid iron. She bent over, cradling her elbow. She waited for the pain to travel to her nerve centers and back. "Shit! My funny bone."

"That was the right idea," SK said, laughing. "But this isn't the best place to learn. If anyone ever touches you again, that's what you do. And don't be shy about poking an attacker in the eyes or kneeing him in the balls or jabbing your finger in his ears or kicking him in the shins. Remember: hard-soft. That's the key."

The pain in Summer's elbow began to ebb. Now it was just an intense tingling and gnawing ache. "If I haven't broken anything, I'm sure I'll be better off for the experience."

Summer could see why SK had developed a following. When they had first met, Summer dismissed her as another edgy feminist hell-bent on flipping the male world on its back. But there was much more to her; a center, a balance that Summer envied. Without her usual armor of hostile self-protection, SK had a commanding air reinforced by an unexpected glimmer of compassion.

"But security isn't your only issue," SK said. "There's something you're hiding. I'd guess it goes way back."

"If I don't get to work on your opening statement—"

"Were you abused as a child?"

"No. Not that I know."

SK cocked her head and smiled. "Not that you know of? That's revealing."

"I mean, I don't have memories from before the age of four."

"Why do you think that is?"

"I don't know."

"What's your first memory?"

"I've had enough excitement for one day."

"It's clear you have a lingering problem with something that happened when you were young," SK said. "Don't you want to find out what's eating away at you?"

"Yes," Summer said, surprising herself. Suddenly, a wave of images cascaded through her. She felt an unbearable sense of fear and abandonment. "My first memory is being sick."

"Tell me," SK said.

Summer tried to hold herself together. She said in a remote voice, "I'm in the entry way of our house, and it's decorated with hundreds of tiny mirrors, from floor to ceiling. And I'm just a little kid, four, I guess, and I'm sick to my stomach, throwing up all these strawberries my father gave me. I look into the mirror and I see red all over, like blood, and it scares me even more because I think it was the first time I ever saw my reflection."

"Where were your parents?" SK asked.

Summer strained for a clearer vision of the memory. "Oh, God, I'd forgotten."

"What is it?"

Summer started to speak, but couldn't put the words together. She coughed.

"Tell me what's on your mind, Summer." SK spoke softly but insistently.

"Sonia comes over and hugs me and says, 'There, there, it's going to be all right. Mommy is here.' But I know she's not my mother." The fact that Marsalis was right about this sends a shock of fear through her.

The door bolt shot back and Sprague entered.

Summer fell to her knees and dry heaved into the bars.

PART IV

TRIAL AND TERROR

CHAPTER 22

INSIDE JUDGE HIGHTOWER'S COURT, the outside world ceased to exist. Summer sat at the defense table with SK, waiting for Raines to begin his opening statement. She was exhausted, adrenaline-rushed and fuzzy-headed from a pot hangover. She had spent the time between leaving SK in the lockup and going home trying to shake the memories loose. But no matter how hard she had tried, she couldn't recall what had happened to her before meeting Sonia for the first time.

Since Summer had been thinking about her opening statement for weeks, it had taken only a few of hours to craft it. At 10 p.m., restless, she'd taken the urn holding Sonia's ashes, driven to the lake where Sonia had drowned, and spread her remains. But a wind had whipped up, and the ashes were blown back into Summer—as if even in death, Sonia would never let go.

Afterward, Summer cursed herself for not having had Sonia's DNA tested before cremation to determine whether she was her mother. But grief and confusion had taken their toll: It simply hadn't occurred to her.

She returned home at midnight but was too wired to sleep. At 2:00, after tossing and turning, the waves outside her windows rumbling at high tide, she swept up crumbs of marijuana that Rosie had spilled at a long-ago party and inexpertly rolled them into a joint, along with dust, sand, and stray hairs. It sizzled and glowed burnt-orange when she lit it, but as rank as it tasted, it knocked her out, although she felt so humiliated by her need to self-medicate that she promised herself never again.

Her last thoughts before copping REM were, *Does Marsalis know who my real mother is? Could I convince him to help me find her?*

There was an anticipatory buzz in the courtroom. SK was meditating with her eyes shut. She wore a dress that Summer had scrounged from friends and shoes from Goodwill. The dress flattered her knife-thin build. She looked more like an upper-middle class mother who spent afternoons at the health spa than the best hand-to-hand fighter in the courthouse.

Summer checked out the jury, a gaggle of distant faces: the retired minister, his creamy-white cheeks spotted with raspberry acne, was doodling; the Libertarian whistled quietly through his teeth; Robinson sat up straight, scanning the courtroom with interest. Others sat impassively; some appeared intimidated, a few seemed bored. Experience had taught Summer that jurors made up their mind during the opening statements. She rifled through her notes and corrected a typo.

All rose for Judge Hightower, who by his sheer size and bearing commanded respect. He scrutinized the courtroom and the jury, and then said, "Mr. Raines, are you ready to give your opening statement?"

"Yes, Your Honor." Raines stood, smoothed his suit, and approached the jury. He pulled a small alarm clock out of his pocket and placed it on the railing. As he spoke, his words were accompanied by a muffled ticking.

"What we have here is a case of revenge—vengeance wrought upon a man for doing his job," he said, his words echoing. "That man, Harold Gundy, is now dead, and this woman, Stephanie Killington, who refers to herself as 'SK,' killed him." Raines pointed to SK and tried to meet each juror's gaze. The implicit message: *I have the courage to look her in the eye and accuse her of murder. Will you have the courage to convict her?*

"Harold Gundy was a respected pillar in this community. He prosecuted some of the most difficult and important cases this county has ever known. Sometimes, people did not agree with his decisions. This, ladies and gentlemen, is the crux of this case."

Summer felt SK shift her chair. She put her hand on her knee: *Stay still, be impassive, be strong.*

Raines continued: "The defendant was once married to a man who earned his living performing abortions."

Summer was about to object: What SK's late husband did for a living was not pertinent and clearly prejudiced the jury—she could see some jurors take notes; already flecks of distaste marred their faces. But to object during opening statements was a major breach of protocol, not to mention the fact that jurors would infer that Summer was trying to cover up information, which she was. She kept mum.

"Now," Raines said, "we are not here to pass judgment on that, no matter how disturbing we may find it. But I tell you this because, eight years ago, another man, Jack Brauer, took it upon himself to kill this doctor. Now this was a tragedy, we all can agree. Harold, heeding the advice of a court-appointed psychiatrist, agreed to a plea of not guilty by reason of insanity and took it upon himself to help Mr. Brauer get the help he needed. He had him committed to the State psychiatric facility.

"But the defendant"—Raines gestured dramatically, scornfully, toward SK—"was not satisfied with this judgment. She threatened Harold's life, and I know this worried him, because as his friend and colleague, I know that whenever hate was directed toward him, it hurt him."

Summer resisted the urge to roll her eyes.

Raines continued. "The defendant swore she would kill Harold the minute Mr. Brauer was released from the hospital. Well, ladies and gentlemen, two days after he left the hospital to take up his life in civilized society again, two days, Harold Gundy was found brutally murdered in his apartment."

Raines was giving the performance of his life. For the first time, Summer realized how much Raines missed Gundy, how the fact that one of his own was killed meant he himself was vulnerable. As sure as Summer was that SK was not the murderer, Raines was sure she was.

"During the course of this trial, we the prosecution will show you irrefutable evidence that this woman murdered Harold Gundy." Raines counted each point off his fingers. "One: The defendant's fingerprints were found on the front door of Harold's home. Two: A fragment of glass from Harold's shattered coffee table was found on one of the defendant's boots in her home. Three: On that glass, the police found blood matching Harold's. Four: Probably the most damning evidence—the defendant brought with her pictures of her husband from the time of his murder on which she had scribbled a message to

Harold. Just before dying, what did Harold see? Why, the pictures, a clue to help the police catch this menace to society. He clutched them to his heart."

Raines let his words sit for a moment. The clock ticked.

"Harold was like that. It is no surprise to anyone who knew him that his last act in this world would be to help the police convict his murderer. That is how he spent his life. That is how he spent his last breath."

The alarm on the clock went off. Raines let the ringing hang in the air, then shut it off.

"Nine minutes. That's how long it took me to tell you about the facts of this case, and that is how long it took the defendant to murder Harold. She knocked on his door, pushed her way in, and forced him upstairs to his second-floor loft. Harold probably tried to defend himself, but the defendant is a black belt in martial arts, and Harold was thrown from the second floor, breaking the railing and crashing into a glass coffee table. But this wasn't enough to kill him and didn't sate her desire for vengeance that day. The defendant dragged Harold a few feet, turned him on his stomach, and beat him over the head with a bottle of liquor. Then, in an attempt to confuse the police by making them think a serial murderer was on the loose, she drew a sign on Harold's back.

"When the killer left the apartment, and we have an eye witness who will verify this, she ran away into the night, hopped a fence like the athlete she is, and sped away.

"Defense counsel is going to try to confuse you, ladies and gentlemen. Be prepared for this. Don't let her lead you down false paths. She may tell you that a crazed murderer is on the loose, or that the defendant was framed, or perhaps that the police didn't investigate other leads. Please, ladies and gentlemen, please ask yourself this: Would a dying man lie to you? Harold had the strength to point out his murderer to you; will you have the strength and wisdom to convict her?"

Fragile silence in the courtroom. When Raines sat down, Hightower's voice cracked with emotion. "Ms. Neuwirth, your opening statement, please."

Summer was unnerved by the power of Raines's performance. She took a sip of water and rose to face the jury.

"Ladies and gentlemen, I'm sorry I don't have any props: no alarm clocks, no plot gleaned from an Agatha Christie murder mystery. How am I to answer this eloquent yet cruel twisting of fact and fiction? How are my client and I to respond to the fact that the case the prosecution has constructed is based on innuendo, circumstantial evidence loosely tied together in some bundle and bumble of information, information that is largely irrelevant to this case?

"How," she gestured with her hands, "are we to address these charges? To start, let me begin with the concept of reasonable doubt, something the prosecution does not want you to know about, because they don't believe you *can* distinguish between fact and fiction. The best analogy I know is a football game. The prosecution has the ball and is driving down the field. To win the game, they have to score a touchdown. The clock is ticking, time is running out, and the ball is on the one-yard line. There's time for one last play. The prosecution hands the ball off and the runner is stopped a half-inch from the goal line. Does the prosecution win? No, they do not. They have not scored. And that, ladies and gentlemen, is the standard of reasonable doubt. The prosecution must prove to you that my client committed this heinous crime. Not get close to proving it, not kind of prove it, but *prove* it to you. Reasonable doubt is a precious standard, difficult to achieve." Summer made eye contact with Robinson. This next part was for her. "If you, by the end of this trial, *think* my client committed this brutal crime, then you must, under our laws, vote *not* guilty. If you are pretty sure my client committed this act, then again, you must vote not guilty. If you think there's a good chance she did it, again, not guilty. Why? Because there is room for doubt. And if any of you are ever charged with a crime you didn't commit, like my client has been, then you will bless the founders of our nation for providing this standard.

"Now, some facts for you to consider.

"Fact: Stephanie did take issue that out of more than a thousand cases in his career, Harold Gundy pleaded a case down to guilty by reason of insanity exactly once. And that was with my client's late husband. Of course she was angry with him, and had, in a state of mourning, said angry things. But that was eight years ago. Have any of you ever said anything in anger only to cool down later?"

Although Summer knew she was handing Raines motive, this was an opportunity to temper its impact, since Raines would undoubtedly introduce the Sadbury murder photos into evidence.

"Fact: Stephanie did drop off pictures at Harold Gundy's residence. In fact, she taped them to his door earlier that day. Hence her fingerprints on the door. But the police didn't find any traces of her *inside* the apartment. No strands of hair. No fingerprints. Nothing. They found plenty of other trace evidence belonging to a number of different women. Blonde hairs, brown hairs, black hairs, but no red hairs. And as you can see, my client has red hair. If Mr. Gundy struggled as the prosecution claims, you'd think she'd have lost a strand or two of hair, maybe cracked a fingernail.

"Fact: Stephanie has had a hard life. She's been an important figure in Haze County." Summer tried to connect with each juror. Some met her gaze, some turned away. Resurrection. A theme they could all relate to. "She took her own money and built a community center for battered women, set up a rape-crisis hotline, a daycare for children so that women on welfare could get off the dole and find jobs. Stephanie has spent hundreds of thousands of dollars of her own money on this, her life's work. In fact, that is why she has me, a public defender, for her lawyer instead of some hotshot private attorney. She's plowed all her money into serving the community and has little left for herself. This is the kind of woman she is. Not a cold, calculated murderer.

"As for her martial arts skills, she teaches women how to defend themselves because for too long women have been the victims of abuse." Summer stopped herself from telling the jury that as someone who was once raped herself, she wished she had known how to defend herself.

"Stephanie has made a difference to everyone she's touched. Besides, ladies and gentlemen of the jury, would anyone, would you, or you, or you"—pointing to the jurors in succession—"be stupid enough to murder someone, then leave behind incriminating pictures? Would you allow yourself to be seen visiting someone in the afternoon, then return later that evening to murder him?"

Summer stopped to catch her breath. "It doesn't add up. By the time this trial is over, you will have no choice but to acquit my client. The police and prosecution need a scapegoat, someone they can blame for a murder they can't solve. But listen carefully, because I'm going to show you that this irrefutable evidence the prosecution talks about is not only refutable, it is a sham."

Summer nodded to Robinson and to the rest of the jury. She returned to the defense table.

But she knew Raines had blown her out of the water.

CHAPTER 23

SUMMER AND ROSIE WERE SITTING on plastic chairs, Summer munching Cuban rice and beans and Rosie *pollo asado* at a one-stop shopping joint in the barrio. The floor was coated in faded linoleum, the edges by the wall curling upward. Tinny salsa music blared through wall-mounted speakers. At the cash register in front, customers could buy condoms and cigarettes one at a time; in the back, crack cocaine and marijuana. But you needed a membership card for that, Rosie explained.

Summer watched Rosie stab half a lemon with a fork and dribble juice over sliced avocado. She didn't know why Rosie, after her initial refusal, had decided to help her find Ignacio, but was relieved that the gulf between them seemed to be closing. Rosie had called Summer right after court was adjourned. That was Friday. Today was Sunday. Aware of Summer's reluctance to wander around Rosie's old neighborhood on her own, she had even insisted on picking her up.

The place catered to the entire Latin community, offering

all kinds of goods and services, legal and illegal. A family sat around a nearby table. Every time the child squalled, the parents shoved food and toys at him until he quieted. A desk on the side offered mini-bus rides to the airport and bus station. Crack addicts, their heads hanging low, skittered to the rear for a fix. Teens rifled through racks of cheap electronics and accessories. Shirtless old men in nylon shorts and cheap sandals bought cans of beer one at a time and sauntered outside to pass their lives.

Rosie shimmied in her chair, waving her knife and fork. "Ray Barretto, the king of the congas," she said. "I love him, even though he was Puerto Rican." She sang along with the lyrics.

"I didn't know they had salsa—music, I mean, in Mexico," Summer said.

"They don't, but that doesn't mean I wasn't raised with it here."

Spicy percussion, unintelligible lyrics, argumentative brass, and grumbling bass. Salsa was Latin culture to Summer. Chaos on the surface, but underneath, a strict structure, a pecking order. That's what Rosie always told her.

Summer talked over the music. "What made you change your mind about helping me find Ignacio?"

"I shouldn't have said 'no' to begin with," Rosie said. "It's not like you could come here and ask around, right? Besides, she wasn't that hard to locate."

"How did you find her?"

"Listen to that." Rosie put down her silverware and clapped out a syncopated pattern. "That's the clavé rhythm, actually a reverse clavé. It's the blood and guts of salsa. Even when you don't hear it explicitly, it's always there. That's how I found Ignacio. I know the rhythms of the neighborhood. I know who she talks to, where she buys food, who watches her kids, who she sleeps with. Most importantly, I know where she gets her fix." With her thumb, Rosie indicated the crackheads in the back.

Summer squirted hot sauce on her beans. "How do you know she'll come in today?"

"Elementary, my dear Summer," Rosie said. "Today, Ignacio will drop her kid off at Sunday school, and she'll come by to pick up some crack, maybe score a client for a nooner. The only question I had was whether she'd skipped town or not. Word is, she's here."

The waiter came over and Summer, in mangled Spanish, ordered a *café con leche.*

"*Dos.*" Rosie covered the chicken bones with a napkin and pushed her plate away. She pulled out a cigarette and lit up. Although the city council had banned smoking in restaurants, nobody paid attention. Rosie blew a lazy cloud of smoke and smiled. "This is fun. Kind of like old times."

Summer treaded carefully. "We haven't done this for a long time. You know, hang out."

Rosie nodded. Summer waited while Rosie flicked ashes onto her plate. "I've been meaning to tell you something."

"What, that because Jon assigned me SK's case you acted like a bitch?" Summer said brutally. "Forget it."

Rosie chewed on her lip. "OK. If it'll make you feel better, go ahead and curse me. I'm a big girl. I can take it."

Summer scooped up the last forkful of beans and regarded them; then dropped the fork on her plate. "It's tough to go through the hard times without your best friend."

"I let you down."

"But why?"

"Listen, what I'm going to tell you, you can't tell anyone."

"*Digame.*"

"Not bad." Rosie put out her cigarette. "Look. You ever do something so bad you couldn't tell anyone?"

Summer didn't say anything. She didn't have to.

Rosie went on. "That's a stupid question. You always do the right thing. But me, well, I've had to make compromises along the way. See that haggard chick with the sores all over her legs, the one hanging with the other crackheads? She lives for the pipe. It's all she wants. That could be me."

"You got out."

"Not without paying a price." She leaned back when the waiter dropped off their coffees. When he left, she grabbed the sugar and poured a mound on top of the foam and watched it sink. "I never told you this, but my old man is in jail. He's a lifer. When I was eight, he took a shot at a pusher but hit a classmate of mine in the eye instead. That's why, as soon as I could, I got out of here. That's why I bought that little house in the white part of town and gave my mother the whole upstairs. I knew it was only a matter of time before the violence or the drugs got to us."

Summer always wondered how on their salaries she could have afforded it. She blew on her coffee to cool it. "Before that, you were into the gangs."

Rosie absently stroked the scars on her arm. "I guess I've been circling around the point here."

"Check that. You're still in with the Latin Brothers."

Rosie iced Summer with a stare. "Somewhat. How long have you known?"

"Actually, it just occurred to me now, although I should

have figured it out a long time ago. Nice of them to let you re-move the gang emblems from your arm." Summer took a long draw of coffee, let it roll over her tongue and down her gullet. "This is delicious coffee, very aromatic."

"*Gracias, El Exigente.* What do you mean, you should have figured it out long ago?"

Summer settled the cup on its saucer, splashing some cof-fee. "Every time I brought up running an investigation, you did your damnedest to dissuade me. You're as gutsy a lawyer as there is. You never back down. It just wasn't your M.O., you know? As I sit here now, it occurs to me that you didn't want me peeling back the layers because I might find you at the core."

"If you're asking, I didn't kill Gundy, OK?"

"But it's clear the boys in the gang wanted Gundy gone, right?"

"I'm not privy to their deepest, darkest secrets, but yeah, that's what I heard. I also heard they didn't get to him because someone else did."

"Are you sure?" Summer asked carefully.

"I'm sure. But if you're thinking of angling your investiga-tion in their direction, I would strongly recommend that you reconsider, because—"

"Because I could end up like Gundy?"

"Don't do this."

"Why can't you just quit? Is that such a naive question?"

"No, it's not, but I'm in too deep. They paid my college tu-ition; law school, too. In exchange, they get a feisty advocate who knows the system inside out and free legal advice for the asking. That's the totality of my connection with them."

"Gundy knew, didn't he?" Summer couldn't look Rosie in the eye.

"I honestly don't know." Rosie tapped three quick fingers on the table. "Hey, Ignacio at three o'clock."

Summer looked left. Ignacio had just entered. She had lost weight in all the wrong places and she had puffy, blow-up doll lips, as if she had been beaten. She had looked toil-worn in jail, but now she looked like she'd taken a few more steps toward her final exit.

"I'll get her." Rosie intercepted Ignacio before she hit the drug store. After a peppery discussion, Rosie brought her over.

Ignacio's perfume preceded her. She sat down, sullen, and crossed her legs, which were branded by bluish veins and cellulite.

"How's your kid?" Summer asked.

Ignacio softened slightly. She might be a crackhead, but Summer could tell she really did love her son. "OK. The school called and said he played hooky, so I smacked him. *Mira.* I don't want him ending up like me."

She said it matter-of-factly, which broke Summer's heart.

Rosie said, "Tell Summer what you saw the night Gundy got popped."

Ignacio looked at the scraps of food on the table. "Could you get that shit out of here? Makes me sick, you know?"

Summer bussed the plates to a nearby cart. "So?" she asked after she sat down.

Ignacio said, "Like I told you in jail, I saw a woman run out of Gundy's."

"She carrying anything?" Rosie asked.

"Yeah, a garbage bag."

Summer and Rosie snuck a glance at each other. This was new.

"When you saw the woman leave Gundy's, what kind of shoes was she wearing?" Summer asked.

"Shoes? Pumps. No heels. Comfortable but classy. Black."

"She wasn't wearing boots?"

"No way."

"You sure?"

"Yeah, yeah, I'm sure," Ignacio said, her voice edged with irritation.

"What color was her hair?"

"Brown, but she was wearing a wig."

"How do you know?"

Ignacio gave off an acidic laugh. "In my business, you gotta know wigs. Fucked up fantasies for all."

"What else you notice?" Summer asked. "Was she white? Black? Tall, short, fat, thin?"

"She was white, thin, but I only saw her from the back. Can't say how tall. She was moving fast."

"If she was wearing a wig, how do you know it wasn't SK?"

Ignacio chose a toothpick from a cup on the table and worked it between her teeth. She made a sucking noise, then said, "SK is too skinny and not so tall."

Summer's forehead was burning. Although she was full, her stomach felt pumped with helium. "Will you testify?"

"No fucking way," Ignacio said. "I don't owe you shit. You didn't get me out."

Rosie slapped the table. "What the fuck? I was your lawyer and the D.A. dropped the charges. Case closed. You owe me, so you owe Summer."

Ignacio rolled her shoulders with attitude and said, "I don't owe nobody nothing, 'cause you didn't lose the file."

Summer whispered, "Who did?"

Ignacio looked around and shook her head.

"*Who?*" Summer's voice lapped over Rosie's.

"Look," Ignacio reasoned stubbornly, "all I know is, you didn't get me out."

Rosie attacked in Spanish. To Summer, their conversation sounded like horn-mad salsa broken up by the occasional "No!" and "Look!" and "Fuck your mother!" Ignacio started out matching Rosie's anger, but eventually backed down.

"Awright, awright," Ignacio said. "Damn, Rosie! The fucking cops know you running with the Latin Brothers? Look, all's I know is, I got sprung and went home and this fucking guy's waiting for me. He has a gun and tells me, I testify, he's going to make sure it's the last thing I ever do."

"What's he look like?" Summer asked.

"Part Chink, Jap maybe," Ignacio told her. "I can smell cop, and this guy was definitely cop. So I ain't testifying. I gotta kid to think about."

CHAPTER 24

Rosie dropped Summer off, after which she called Tai's answering service and was told he was rock climbing at the Ocean Spa Gym.

After paying an entrance fee and hiking past an Olympic-sized swimming pool; a track; basketball, squash, and tennis courts; a weight room; and various types of aerobics classes, she spotted him, sweaty and shirtless, peering up at the top of an artificial rock face marked with nooks, crannies, and plastic pegs.

He was adjusting his safety harness when Summer clamped a hand on his shoulder.

"What the—" he turned. When he saw it was Summer, he gave her an exaggerated smile. "Hey! I was going to call you. I just got back."

Summer slapped him.

Tai stood there without a reaction, his smile intact. "What? Did I forget your birthday?"

Summer tried to temper her anger. "Why did you threaten Ignacio and tell her not to testify?"

"Ohhhh," he revved. "That's why you're mad."

"That's right," Summer said. "Before I fire you, I want to know why you've been interfering with my investigation."

He twisted his mouth into a smirk. "Your investigation? You don't know the first thing about investigating. The person who murdered Gundy is right under your nose and you don't see it. But OK. I'm fired."

He turned his back on her and started up the wall.

Summer grabbed his shorts. The elastic waistband snapped back when he pulled free. She called after him. "Don't give me that cryptic shit. I'm paid to defend my clients, and if SK says she's innocent, then I have to do my damnedest to get her off."

Tai was already up ten feet. He stopped and looked down. "I'm not talking about SK."

Summer watched him continue up the wall. "I'm not done with you," she said.

Tai didn't answer. He was carefully working his way up. As he ascended, a man at the top pulled the rope taut. Tai's arms and back were pumped with blood, his muscles straining and defined.

"Tai!" she shouted.

Tai slipped momentarily but hung on.

Summer could feel her pulse pound at her temples. And the farther away Tai got, the harder her blood beat and the more her forehead boiled. Before she knew what she was doing, she'd kicked off her shoes, sending them flying into the wall, and started after him.

The man at the top cupped his hands and yelled down. "Yo, dude, dudette, whatever. It's not cool without a safety harness."

Summer shut him out of her brain. She placed the arch of her foot on a tiny crag and her hand on a peg and pulled herself up. Plagued by a severe fear of heights, she resisted the urge to look down, and instead focused on Tai, who was contemplating his next move.

The man at the top warned her he would call security. Summer's lungs were beginning to ache. Her hands were slippery with sweat. She wished she had gloves like Tai. But she kept on, closing the gap on Tai, who looked down at her with alarm.

"Summer, what are you doing?" he said.

"I told you, I'm not done with you." She rested her forehead against the wall for a moment, and then continued upward.

"OK, you win," Tai said. "You can get down now."

Summer ignored him like he had ignored her. She moved sideways a few steps to follow a course parallel to his. Her arms were shaking, but she urged herself on. She was more than halfway. Coming down would be far worse, she reasoned. Better to get to the top and take the elevator from the mezzanine.

"Those floor mats are pretty skinny," Tai said. "If you fall, you could die. At the very least, you'll break something."

Summer took it one plastic rock, one movement, at a time. A wave of nausea passed over her. She took deep breaths until it passed. Even though she had slowed down, she was still closing in on Tai. She was close enough to smell his sweat. Her mind was wandering. She snapped back to attention. One foot slipped off. She frantically held on.

There were "oohs" from below. She glanced down and saw that a crowd had gathered. She struggled to plant her foot.

Tai said, "You have nerve, I'll give you that much."

"Are you working for the D.A., is that it?" She tried not to let her voice quiver. "Is that why you intimidated my only eye-witness?"

"You've got it all wrong."

"Like hell I do. What did they offer you? A chance to get off disability and get back on the force? A promotion? I mean, how disabled can you be if you can climb walls?"

"First of all, I've learned how to compensate for my injury. Second, you're ready to convict me without knowing the facts."

He was a ten feet from the top, and Summer was five feet behind him. She shrugged off the dizzies. "All I know is that you ran from me when I confronted you."

"SK ran from the cops, and you're *defending* her."

Summer was in an awkward position, the toes of one foot wrapped around a tiny jut, her fingers clawing a slight serra-tion. The wall's angle got steeper the closer she got to the top. She should have taken a different route.

Tai hoisted himself over the top. He leaned over and of-fered her his hand. "Just a few more feet and you're home free."

Summer didn't think she could go another step. She was afraid she was going to black out. At least that way she wouldn't feel the impact when she hit the ground.

Tai shouted. "C'mon, Summer. Move it! The longer you stay on the wall, the less time we'll have to talk over dinner."

She was too weak to tell him that the last incentive she needed was a date with him.

There was a rush of activity above. She heard Tai tell someone, "Keep the rope taut. I'm going after her."

Summer prepped for a final run at the top, but a child-hood memory pierced her. The minutes before meeting Sonia for the first time: *She's in the car with Wib and he's comforting her, telling her, "I know you're too young to understand this, but you're so much better off with us. It's also better for your mother." He's feeding her strawberries, juicy and sweet. Bribery for good behavior.*

There was hope. All the information lay within her, not with Marsalis. Maybe she could figure it all out without his help. She cleared her mind and began to finish the climb, tailing away from a descending Tai.

She ignored the hands hanging down, and with one last shot of energy, willed herself over the ledge. Safe now, she collapsed, barely aware of the circle of concerned faces over her.

"Should we call the police?" someone asked.

"I am the police," Tai said, "and no. Don't. Give her some air. I'll take care of this." When no one moved, he yelled, "Scram! Except you—" He pinched the collar of one man's shirt. "Get her some water."

The group dispersed.

Summer's breathing was steadying.

Tai said, "I have never met anyone like you before, Summer Neuwirth. You are really something."

She tried to sit up, but Tai pinned her shoulders.

"Rest easy," he said.

After drinking almost a liter of water and eating a Power Bar she felt better. They sat on the edge of the wall, their feet hanging over, Tai still in his safety harness.

"You're going to be sore tomorrow," he said.

"Not as sore as I'll be if you don't have a good explanation for Ignacio."

"I'll tell you why I did what I did. After you hear me out, if you still feel you should fire me, I'll save you the trouble and quit."

"I'm listening."

"I found out the D.A. was onto Ignacio. She made the mistake of yakking in prison and one of her cell stooges passed it on. I went to the jail and what do I discover? You visited her. Big mistake, Summer. If I found out you talked to her, then the D.A. could too. Right then, I knew I had to get her out: You know bad things can happen inside. I arranged for her file to disappear, got her out of there, and went to see her."

"And all that time I thought you were in Birch Creek."

"Yeah, well," Tai said, "I didn't want you getting mixed up in this. You've got enough to worry about. You know, if you put Ignacio on your witness list, Raines is gonna bring the law down hard on her. At best, get her to recant on the stand. At worst, make her change her story, totally fuck up your case. He's playing hardball and will do anything to win. Don't you get it? The dudes who control Haze County can't afford for the D.A. to blow another one. Marsalis was bad enough, but a murder with incomplete police work, maybe incompetence, will make the whole criminal justice system look like it's out of control. I had to put the fear of God in Ignacio, keep her from blowing it, ruining your case; hell, maybe getting you in trouble. If Raines could get her to testify that you tried to spring her illegally, you'd be up to your crystal blue eyes in shit."

Summer couldn't believe how close she had come to losing everything. Hot and flushed, less from the climb up the wall now than humiliation, she swished water around her mouth and swallowed. *Steady*, she told herself. "Why go to all this trouble?"

"To protect you," he said simply. "Because we're really not that different. We've both been fucked over by the system. Me, I lost the one job I loved. And you, you're dangerously close to blowing this case, letting an innocent women die for someone else's deeds. I couldn't let that happen."

Summer rubbed her eyes. "I can't believe I did this. I just want to win so badly... *have* to win this case, that I lost control." She was afraid to ask, but... "You said the murderer was right under my nose."

He leveled his gaze at her. "Under your nose and right next door. You've worked with her for four, five years."

"Rosie? You're telling me that Rosie murdered Gundy? No way."

Tai played with the straps of his harness. "She had motive, opportunity, and no alibi, plus she fits Ignacio's description. She's tight with Miguel de Libertad, the gang's *queso grande*. He took over for Juan Ponce, who's doing 25 to life. And who put him there? Gundy. These gangbangers aren't stupid. They know if they axed Gundy in traditional gangland style, the cops would go to war. So why not kill him a different way, make sure the trail doesn't lead to them? And who better than a woman? With his twisted sexual needs? Damn right. And you know how much Rosie hated Gundy."

"She wasn't the only one," Summer said opaquely.

"True, but Rosie would be smart enough to recognize an opportunity when she saw it. She's a lawyer. She knows how a police investigation is conducted. She took advantage of the fact that pictures of SK's murdered husband would make ironclad evidence."

"But she couldn't be sure that SK didn't have an alibi."

"Which is why she also threw in the lipstick symbol, another red herring. Anything to keep the scent off her—and the Latin Brothers."

"If Rosie had anything to do with Gundy's death, why

would she help me track down the only one who could identify her?"

"What makes you think Ignacio was telling the truth? She's no Mother Theresa. Even if she was telling the truth, it was dark and she probably didn't get a good look."

"Still, if what you say is true, then Ignacio, since she can ID the murderer, is in grave danger."

"Probably not. I'd bet the gang leadership wants Ignacio alive. Great insurance policy. Keep Rosie in line for years to come." Tai coughed. "You going to cover for her?"

"She didn't do it."

"But if she did?"

Summer worked her neck around to get rid of the kinks. "I don't know."

"I never expected you to follow me up this wall," Tai said. "You're full of surprises."

"So are you."

"You want to grab a bite to eat?"

Summer thought it over. "OK. I'll meet you downstairs."

"Where are you going?" He was still sitting.

"I'm not going anywhere. You are."

From behind she shoved him with her foot. He balanced precariously for a moment, then slid off. He screamed her name as he plummeted. When the rope pulled taut, he was yanked upward, then plunged downward again, until he was hanging 15 feet off the ground, rumbling with laughter.

CHAPTER 25

THEY DIDN'T GO TO DINNER. Yet.

Tai had jogged to his workout, so Summer drove him home where he could shower and change.

He lived in a shy A-frame with a porch and side garden. Incandescent flowers in white, orange, and red with black hearts bloomed around cacti and basil and tomatoes and squash. Tai opened the screen door.

Summer asked, "What kind of flowers are those? They're beautiful."

"Poppies." Tai removed his shoes and left them by the door.

Summer flicked hers off, too. "As in opium poppies?"

"All poppies have some opium in them. It's only illegal if you slit the heads open and try to manufacture narcotics. Then the DEA could come calling and that would suck. All the DEA has to do to confiscate your home and all your assets is merely accuse you of a drug crime." He ushered her inside. "If you want, I could brew some opium tea—now that's illegal, but who's going to find out?"

"No thanks. I thought that opium poppies only grew in the Golden Triangle, like Thailand and Burma. Where did you get them? "

"I grew them from seeds, which you can buy anywhere, even at Woolworth's. The DEA has been waging a campaign of misinformation for decades, propagating the myth that these poppies can't grow in American soil. The Northeast has the best climate for them. Imagine if everyone knew. They'd be harvesting opium by the ton in New Jersey."

While Tai threw himself in the shower, Summer puttered around. She would have never imagined his house to look this way. Throw rugs from Mexico and Kashmir blended into one another and partially covered the oak floor. A few pieces of abstract art hung on the walls, and a faint scent of sandalwood and cedar mingled in the air.

A few minutes later she heard him rustle in the bedroom.

"Your home is very elegant," she called.

He emerged wearing black drawstring pants and a collarless button down shirt, his hair freshly tousled. "Unlike me," he said. "You want something to drink?"

"OJ?"

"In the kitchen."

Tai had a cast-iron stove, gleaming appliances, a built-in butcher block, and a hand-crafted table. Summer sat down while Tai grabbed a couple handfuls of oranges and began slicing them. "This was my parents' house, but my father left to open a jazz club in Tokyo. My mom really wanted to go home."

"You're half-Japanese," Summer said.

Tai tossed a bad orange in the trash. "On my mom's side. My old man is a mix of everything—all the scum of Eastern Europe washed up in one body."

"Stalin, right?"

"Right. And you?"

Summer measured her words. "I'm not sure. A mix, too."

He juiced the oranges a half at a time, poured the liquid into tall glasses and joined Summer at the table. "*Kampai*," he said. "That means 'cheers.' "

She drank. "Mmmm. And I was expecting plain old store-bought."

"Your dad was a cop," Tai said. "Wib Neuwirth, right?"

"Uh-huh."

"He was set to retire when I graduated from the academy. He was lionized by everyone."

"He was a good man." Summer took another sip. She was beginning to feel stiff, especially her shoulders and neck.

"I think you should move in here," Tai said casually.

Summer dropped the glass on the table. As it rolled toward the edge, she tried to grab it, but accidently flicked it off the table instead. It shattered, showering the floor with juice.

"I got it." Tai ripped off a few sheets of paper towel. He picked up the shards and cleaned up the juice. Then got out his dust-buster to suck up any stray splinters. "I'm not asking you to move here because I can't live without you—at least not yet. It's for your own safety."

"That's a novel approach."

"It's not an approach. Take a look at this." He stepped to a shelf and brought over a 1954 Birch Creek High School yearbook. "Page 96, check out graduating senior Elaine Stockton."

Summer flipped it open and located Stockton's picture. She

looked at it, then up at Tai, then down at the picture again. Stockton was blonde, with an athletic build and a very familiar face.

"It's uncanny," Summer said.

"Like looking into a mirror, right? I was pretty blown away when I came across it."

"I don't get why this is a threat to my safety... unless... does it have anything to do with Marsalis?"

"You might say that," Tai said. "It's his mother."

Summer pushed her chair away from the table. She stood. Even though she'd thought she was beyond surprise, this knocked her back. "Where is she now?"

"No one knows. She disappeared some time in the late sixties, when Marsalis was a teenager. I talked to some of his childhood acquaintances—he didn't have any friends. No one knows what happened to her."

Summer felt like she had when she'd looked down from the wall. She thought about the circumstances around Sonia's disappearance and subsequent death. But she had disappeared months before Marsalis came into her life.

Tai continued. "Marsalis is a perv, and you know how weird pervs get about their relationships with mommy. I'm sure it isn't lost on him that you are the spitting image of his dearly departed mother. I'm afraid he's going to come after you."

"He already has."

Tai nodded. "So that's why you stopped using your cell phone. I wondered why you always called from your office landline or various blocked cell numbers."

"How did you know the blocked cell numbers came from different phones?"

"How do ya think?"

Summer silently answered her own question: *an ex-cop*

with contacts inside the phone company. She told Tai how Marsalis had been stalking her, and the facts surrounding Sonia's disappearance and subsequent death. But she left out some key points; she wasn't ready to tell Tai everything. She didn't mention her own rape, cruelly reconstructed by Marsalis on the World Wide Web, or the fact that she'd already questioned whether Sonia and Wib were her biological parents. "It's too much of a coincidence that I would be assigned Marsalis."

"Tell me how P.D.s get their cases."

"It's random, unless Jon decides to appoint someone."

"Did Levi appoint you to Marsalis?"

"No, it came down the usual way," Summer said. "Every time I conclude a trial, I tell the paralegal in charge of assignments, and he adds a new client to my case load."

"Who keeps track?"

"Jon, I guess."

"How?"

"He checks the computer files and—Oh, God. Marsalis could have been following me for months," Summer said distantly. "I wonder how he found me."

"He might have spotted you at a café. Or saw you on the beach. He could have come across you any which way. It doesn't matter. You weren't assigned Marsalis. He chose you."

"He said fate brought us together."

"In his twisted mind, he probably meant it was fate that he found you."

Or did Marsalis mean something else entirely? Summer wondered. She studied the picture. "I was hoping you'd discover that Marsalis and Strickland were the same person, or at least find Strickland alive so I could get a jury to buy the idea that he murdered Gundy."

"Strickland is alive."

Before falling, Summer leaned her hands on the back of the chair and slipped her leg around the side. She sat. When Tai made a made to help, she waved him off. "I'm OK."

Tai continued. "Strickland's alive, but no way he murdered Gundy. He has full-blown AIDS, been living in an AIDS hospice. He's bedridden, about to kick the bucket. I saw him."

Summer buried her head into the crook of her arm, muffling her voice. "Then whose body did they find in the car?"

"It belonged to a hitchhiker. Apparently Strickland murdered more people than we thought. The only ones he left calling cards with were in law enforcement, though. A neat little game for him."

Summer wondered what Mahakavi would think of Strickland now. She looked up and sighed. "That means I'm back to trying to shoot holes in the D.A.'s case."

"I'm sorry."

"It's not your fault. You did good work."

"You have, too. I heard what you did during jury selection the other day. If I were still a cop, I'd curse you from here to eternity."

"Kinder words were never spoken. But I got lucky. Next time Raines will be more careful." Summer felt the blood swish around her head. "Can I lie down a few minutes? It's been a rough life—day, I mean."

Tai led her past the living room and slid open some rice-paper doors. She entered a room with mat floors. Tai opened the closet and pulled out a futon, sheets, a blanket, and pillows. He made the bed and Summer crawled into it.

She felt so weak, as if she were leaking through the futon and into the floor. Tai settled himself at a two-foot high table across the room. He squirted hot water through green tea leaves and into a cup and flipped open a laptop, which he rested on his knees. "Gonna catch up on the news," he explained.

Summer watched him read, how he tilted his head when looking at a photo, smiled when something struck him as funny. She took a series of deep breaths, encouraging the oxygen to restore her strength. She realized that even though she was exhausted, knowing Tai was near made her feel safe.

She reached out a hand. "Tai. Could you come here?"

He smiled and shut the lid of the laptop. He uncurled his legs from under the table and approached, squatting near her. "Can I get you anything?" he asked.

She took his hand. "Stay."

While he snuggled beside her, she turned away and they lay, her back to his front. Outside, she could hear birds, a light wind. The first peace she'd had in months. Tai seemed to mold himself to her shape. He was almost weightless. All she could feel of him was his breath, which stuck to the nape of her neck.

She turned toward him and found herself smiling back at him. Their breaths intermingled, the faint scent of orange juice. She ran her hand through his hair. He took it and kissed it gently.

When she pulled him closer for a kiss, he said, "Shhhh. There's no rush, Summer. I'm happy just to be here with you. I don't want you to feel any pressure. I just want you to feel happy, secure."

She leaned into him and they brushed lips, first lightly, then with hunger. She hugged him hard. He whispered, *You're so beautiful*, over and over.

When she felt his fingers lightly skim her back, she said, "Wait."

Tai stopped.

Summer sat up. "I have to show you something."

He sat up with her. "You can tell me anything."

"I was raped, and it left some scars."

Tai waited for her to continue.

"I haven't been with anyone since. So, I want you to see my back before you make up your mind whether you want to be with me."

"It doesn't matter."

"It does to me."

"Tell me what happened."

"Later. First, I want you to see."

She turned away and lifted up her shirt.

"I don't see anything," he said.

"They're there. Look."

She felt him lightly run his hand down her spine. She shivered.

"Summer, the scars are inside you, not on your back. Your back is as smooth and velvety as the rest of you."

She felt a crying jag on the way. She turned and hugged him, overcome with yearning. But this triggered the memories: being blinded, having her insides ripped apart by his savage thrusting, the fear of not knowing whether she would live, the pain when he burned her back with a knife he had heated on the stove.

She pushed Tai off. "I'm sorry. I can't do this."

She rehooked her bra as she ran from the room, away from Tai's pleadings, out to the porch, leaving her shoes behind. She jumped into her truck, flooring it when Tai emerged from the house.

CHAPTER 26

RAINES WAS QUESTIONING THE STATE'S first witness, Detective Doyle Tyler, a thirty-year veteran of the force. He had a small, hard face and a beaky nose, but a body of beef, his suit straining to hold all of him in. He reminded Summer of a kindergartner's drawing, all his parts out of proportion—short arms but hammy hands, wide shoulders but wider waist, eyes that were big and round but too close together.

Lead-off witnesses make the strongest impressions in the minds of juries, which is why detectives, because they spend much their time in court, usually make good ones. But not Tyler. He had a bland personality, not the kind a jury could bond to; he often answered questions without thinking; his record was merely adequate. But he was predisposed to help the prosecution, which was the main reason, Summer assumed, that Raines put him on the stand first.

Originally, Raines had ordered his witnesses differently, beginning with Chantelle Jones, the medical examiner. But

Summer had hammered out an arrangement with Raines: the defense would stipulate to the medical examiner's findings, which meant at a certain point in the trial, Chantelle's testimony would simply be read into the record, as long as an addendum was added stating that other than the fingerprints on the pictures and exterior portion of the door, no other physical evidence—hair fibers, blood, skin cells—tied SK to the crime scene.

For the defense, this defused the power of the evidence, particularly the gruesomeness of the crime, and took away the D.A.'s best witness. The prosecution benefitted as well. Anything could happen when a witness took the stand, especially in the dense realm of medical science, where juries often stumbled over the arcania and missed the important points. Stipulation also meant that the trial would be at least two days shorter, giving Summer fewer opportunities to poke holes in the D.A's case. Taking no chances, Raines had eagerly agreed.

Tyler testified that Hightower's clerk had called the police after Gundy didn't show for the Marsalis verdict. A patrolman found his door unlocked and Gundy's head caved in, blood-stained carpeting, a shattered table, and police photos, some pinned under the body and others strewn about the room. He immediately called homicide. Tyler was the one to respond.

Raines was wearing a designer-brand suit that contrasted with his off-the-rack personality. He set his foundation, questioning Tyler on what the detective had encountered at the crime scene. Tyler said he'd called in the forensics team and they informed him of the fingerprints on the photos and on the lower-left hand corner of the front door. When Tyler had them cross-matched, he discovered that they belonged to Stephanie Killington.

"Are every citizen's fingerprints on file with the police?" Raines asked.

"No," Tyler said.

"Then how is it that the police would have the defendant's fingerprints on file?"

"Fingerprints are kept on file from anyone who is a legal alien, applies for a job with the county, or has a criminal record."

"Which group does the defendant fall into?" Raines asked, fully aware of the answer.

Objection," Summer said. "Irrelevant."

"Well," Hightower drawled, "perhaps not irrelevant, but why don't you find a less broad way to ask that question, Counselor?"

"Certainly," Raines responded. "To your knowledge, Detective Tyler, is the defendant a legal alien?"

"Not to my knowledge."

"Has she ever applied for a job with the county?"

"No, sir."

"Oh," Raines said in mock dramatic fashion. "You mean to say she has a criminal record?"

Summer objected again on the grounds that it would unfairly prejudice the jury. She knew there wasn't a chance her objection would be sustained, but to set up grounds for a possible appeal she had to aggressively object throughout the trial—even at the risk of alienating the jury, who might suspect her of trying to cover up the truth.

"Overruled," the judge said. "You may answer the question."

"Yes," Tyler testified. "The defendant has a criminal record. Prostitution."

It wasn't yet 10 a.m. and Raines had found a way to inject moral impropriety into the minds of the jury.

"How long did it take for you to receive positive identification on these fingerprints?"

"Two days," Tyler answered. "There was a backlog of requests."

"Who else was at the scene with you?"

"The police photographers. I instructed them to take pictures of the crime scene, and I remained there for the duration."

At the beginning of the trial, Summer and Raines had offered arguments as to which pictures should be allowed into evidence. On this point, Hightower was surprisingly squeamish, ruling that only three shots of Gundy's body, including the Jonathan Sadbury crime scene pictures trapped underneath him on which SK had scrawled the word "shame" and one close-up of the fatal head wound, were necessary.

Raines plucked the photos from the evidence cart, showed them to Summer, and then to Tyler, who in a bland monotone described each of the pictures as being accurate representations of the murder scene. Hightower glanced at them and then had Sprague pass them to the jury. There was a lot of blood. Summer could see the retired minister recoil. Robinson, too, blinked in horror.

"Were you suspicious of the defendant before the physical evidence was in?" Raines asked.

Tyler answered dryly. "The victim was holding photos of the defendant's husband when he died. I thought this might be a clue to the identity of his attacker. I was also present when the defendant threatened Mr. Gundy in the past."

This opened the door for Raines to dredge up motive: the Sadbury case, on which Tyler and Gundy had worked together.

Tyler testified that after Gundy let her husband's murderer plead insanity, SK threatened to kill Gundy the day Brauer walked through the gates of the asylum.

"Does Mr. Brauer still reside in the State psychiatric hospital?" Raines asked.

"He was released two days before Mr. Gundy was murdered."

Raines let that soak in. Then he asked, "When you were told the defendant's fingerprints matched those on the victim's front door and on the pictures, what did you do?"

"I got a warrant to search the defendant's home." Tyler told the court how he had shown up at her door with a search team and entered SK's top-floor residence. "The defendant walked in part way through the search."

"What did you find?"

"A pair of boots with a fragment of glass embedded in the sole of one, stained by blood."

"How did the defendant react?"

"She fled." Tyler told the court how SK had surprised him by racing out, jumping a fence, and sprinting into the adjacent woods. Tyler put out a warrant for her arrest and she was collared by police in an abandoned industrial park.

Raines concluded his questioning with: "You have put more than 30 years into being a homicide detective. Is it your experience that innocent people run?"

Summer objected on the grounds that it was speculative.

Hightower took a moment to scroll the testimony on his computer monitor. "Overruled. The witness is being asked for his opinion based on his experience."

"No. Innocent people don't run." Tyler added "in my opinion" for good measure.

Raines turned to Summer. "Your witness, counselor."

Summer took a sip of water and psyched herself for the cross. She summoned her own experiences—the callous way the detectives had treated her rape, the corrupt way some cops had acted, the way they'd lied to cover up their behavior. By the time she approached Tyler, she wanted to obliterate him.

"Detective Tyler," she said, "you just testified that, in your experience, innocent people don't run. Is that correct?"

"Correct." Tyler itched his nose.

"Have you arrested many innocent people?"

"Of course not."

"Then what experiences do you draw on when you say that innocent people don't run?"

Raines jumped up. "Your Honor, the defense is badgering this witness."

"Is there an objection in there somewhere, counselor?" Hightower asked sarcastically. He was a stickler for form, especially at the start of a trial.

"Objection," Raines said automatically.

"Overruled." Hightower used a voice that sounded like "Nah-nah." He was laying down the law in his court: *Object at your own risk.* "The witness is instructed to answer the question."

Tyler shook his head. "Experience? More like logic."

"So, are we to conclude that you based this assumption not on experience but on something else entirely?"

Tyler appeared confused. "I guess you could say that."

"Are you precise with the language you use, Detective Tyler?"

Summer heard Raines start to object but hold back. He was waiting to find out what tack Summer was taking.

"Yeah, sure, I mean, when I'm on the job. When I'm off-duty, I don't really think about it."

"That's fair," Summer said. "So when you said that, based on your experiences that—"

Hightower cut her off. "You've already established this point."

"Sorry, Your Honor," Summer said. "Detective Tyler, you testified that forensics found fingerprints on Mr. Gundy's front door. Correct?"

"Yes."

"Which side? The inside or outside?"

"The outside."

"It doesn't bother you that your earlier testimony implied that the fingerprints were on the inside?"

"I didn't imply anything. I said they found fingerprints on the door."

Summer let it go. She had established that anything Tyler said should be taken with a grain of salt. She changed direction and brought up Tyler's record. He had come up empty on the three cases he had worked on prior to collaring SK. He admitted that the failure to catch these culprits had resulted in intense pressure from his superiors. But after arresting SK, this pressure lessened.

"What are your feelings regarding my client?" Summer asked.

"I have no feelings one way or the other," Tyler responded. "A case is a case, and a suspect is a suspect."

"And you had no feelings regarding my client's late husband, Jonathan Sadbury, and his work, did you?"

"None."

"Nor the fact that he performed abortions?" Since Raines had already worked this nugget into his opening statement, Summer knew she couldn't work around it.

"Right," he said in a clipped voice.

Summer removed a photocopy from a folder. "Do you remember writing a check for $750 to the Anti-Abortion Crusade?"

Tyler was clearly ambushed. Summer had to hand it to Tai. He really did know how to investigate. She let Tyler's silence hang in the air.

"Time's a-wasting, Detective Tyler," Summer said in a noisy whisper. "If you're not careful, you'll anger Mr. Raines. You know what a stickler for time he is. He even carries an alarm clock with him wherever he goes."

Over the laughter, Hightower said, "That's quite enough, Ms. Neuwirth."

"My apologies, Your Honor. Well, Detective Tyler? Yes or no?"

"That was a long time ago," he said.

"Yes, eight years ago, not long before Jonathan Sadbury was slain." She showed him the photocopy. "Is this your signature?"

He fumbled for his eyeglasses. "It is."

"But you're telling the court that you don't have feelings regarding Jonathan Sadbury's work one way or the other. Is that correct?"

"I would never let it affect my judgment on the job."

"I didn't ask that."

"All right," he said. "I'm against abortion and believe Jonathan Sadbury's work was immoral. But that doesn't mean—"

"After Mr. Sadbury was murdered, did you say that God was just evening the score?"

Tyler took a sip of water. He was sweating and his eyes were red. "I don't recollect ever having said that."

"If I could produce a witness who would swear that you had, would he be lying?"

Tyler answered before Raines could object. "I don't know."

Summer withdrew the question. Haze County was in the heart of Right To Life, U.S.A. She wasn't sure how much damage this would cause Raines's case—hell, she thought, three-quarters of the jury probably agreed with Tyler's stance. But she was laying the foundation for their mistrust.

She moved on to the crime scene. "Were you the first one to search the bedroom where the boots were found?"

"No. Another member of the search team had already searched."

"Where was he when you were in the bedroom?"

"In the bathroom."

"Your colleague searched the room?"

"He did."

"And yet it was you who found the boots."

"Yes."

"While he was not present."

"Yes."

"How long were you unsupervised?"

Tyler sucked in some air. "About, oh, five minutes, give or take."

Summer approached him. "You didn't plant evidence, did you, Detective Tyler?"

Tyler's face narrowed. His pupils were little beads. "Absolutely not."

"If you had wanted to, however, it is possible that you could have transported a glass fragment with a drop of blood on it to my client's home and planted it."

"Objection," Raines called. "This is pure fantasy, supposition."

"Overruled," the judge said. "Counselor merely asked the witness whether it was possible to plant evidence if he'd had the desire to. She didn't accuse him."

Tyler said, "I would never do that. It's possible I could have done a lot of things. I could have walked off with the family silver. I could have painted graffiti on her walls. I could have taken a nap. The point is, I didn't."

"I see. Detective Tyler, what else was on the boots?"

"I don't understand the question."

"No, strike that," Summer said. "You testified on direct that Malcolm Byers, the eyewitness you interviewed, offered a description of the clothes worn by someone fleeing the crime scene?"

"Yes."

"Did you ever find these clothes?"

"She could have ditched them."

"If she ditched the clothes, why would she keep the boots?"

"Objection," Raines called. "Calls for speculation."

"I'll rephrase the question. Based on your experiences, why would a suspect ditch some articles of clothing, but not all?"

"Maybe she panicked."

Summer crossed her arms. "She's not the only one."

Raines was up in a flash and barked, "Objection."

Hightower said, "That is unnecessary, Ms. Neuwirth. You've made your point."

"OK," Summer said, "Let's try this. Detective Tyler, you're saying that the boots you found are the boots the killer wore, right?"

"That's logical."

"So you're saying the killer wore the boots, and then stepped on the glass fragments during or after the perpetration of the crime?"

"Yes."

"Then wore these boots all the way to my client's residence?"

"Yes."

"Walked on pavement, up the dirt path leading to the Center's front door?"

"Yes.

"Then why is it that there is no dirt or mud on the soles of the boots?"

Tyler stumbled. "I don't have an answer for that."

Out of the corner of her eye, Summer could see Robinson and some of the other jurors scrawling notes. The electrician held a finger to his lips and seemed to be giving this a lot of thought. The computer magazine editor pursed his lips. *Everybody likes a good fight,* Summer thought. *Good.* They were in for a treat.

She was in a rhythm. "Outside of the victim's home, there's a concrete path, right?"

"Right."

"No other way for the killer to have exited the victim's premises, right?"

"Not that I know of."

"The windows were locked and sealed, and there was no back door, correct?"

"Yes."

"So why do you think the glass fragment doesn't show any wear, no scrapings, nothing?"

Tyler shook his head. "I don't know."

"So let me get this straight. The perpetrator wore a pair of boots, somehow gets a glass fragment with a dab of the victim's blood on it lodged in one of them, wears them the four miles to my client's home, walks or runs over concrete and dirt, but somehow the soles stay pristine?"

"I wouldn't say pristine exactly."

"Oh?" Summer held up the boots and showed the soles. "Pristine, except for this fragment of bloody glass."

"I suppose."

"Is it possible the killer skipped the walking part and drove from the victim's door to the Center's door, or perhaps flew on a magic carpet?"

"She could have driven."

"But forensics, to your knowledge, found no trace of physical evidence in my client's car."

"That's correct."

"Would you say the killer took off his or her boots, put on a different pair to go home, carried them to the Center—yet didn't notice the glass or blood—and deposited them in my client's closet?"

Tyler was nettled. "That's absurd."

"So if you assume the killer wore the boots home, he or she had to walk in them, at least as far as the parking lot."

"I'd say you'd have to assume that."

"Then how do you account for the cleanliness of the soles?"

"I can't."

CHAPTER 27

THE NEXT TWO COURT DAYS were spent criss-crossing over the testimony of a local martial arts instructor, who offered his opinion that SK, from what he could tell from documentary footage, did possess the skills to toss a 220-pound man through a railing; entering Chantelle's medical examiner's report into the record, which, although a dry recitation of the evidence, was extremely damning; and making various motions to Hightower outside the purview of the jury on certain points of evidence.

Normally, when Summer worked a trial, she skipped breakfast, usually too nervous to eat. But today she was ravenous and headed to the cafeteria. She joined the line and grabbed a tray, slowly moving past hot plates containing eggs, waffles, pancakes. She chose cereal, a fruit cup, and coffee, paid for it, and carried her tray out to the sun deck.

Two bites into her meal, a shadow crossed over her.

"Mind if I join you?" Tai asked.

Summer took her briefcase off the chair. "Of course not."

Tai set his tray down, sat next to her and removed his sunglasses. "I caught your act with Tyler the other day. You made him look like the ass he is."

"Thanks," Summer said, taking a bite of canned pineapple. "But even if the jury buys the idea that Tyler planted the bloody glass in the boot, they could easily view it as a cop enhancing evidence to ensure that a murderer is put away."

Tai dug into his scrambled eggs and talked while chewing. "You always so cheerful? Don't answer that. I already know."

"I'm sorry I haven't returned your calls."

Tai swallowed. "I'm the one who should be sorry. I pushed you when I shouldn't have. It's just—"

"I can't do this now."

Tai scraped the eggs off and began tearing off pieces of toast. While he talked, he tossed the crumbs to the birds. "Have you heard from Marsalis recently?"

"Surprisingly, no."

"He's a hard man to track."

Summer's cereal settled into the pit of her stomach. "Leave him alone, Tai. I don't want him riled up."

Tai tossed the last of the bread. "This psycho threatened you and you don't want to rile *him* up? What gives? I can understand why you wouldn't want the cops in on this, but I'm one of the good guys. Remember?"

"You don't know who you're dealing with. He's very dangerous."

Tai gave her a dismissive laugh. "There's something you're not telling me."

"Please stay away from Marsalis."

"And from you, right?"

Summer didn't respond.

"Oh, fuck it." Tai frisbee'ed his plate into the bushes.

Summer snickered.

"Oh, so you don't hate me." Tai said.

She touched his cheek. "Of course not."

He held her hand there for a moment, and then reached into his daypack and extracted a DVD. "Brought you a little gift. Pizza Boy, the D.A.'s only eye witness, is coming up later today, right? Did you know that he was weenie wagger?"

Summer's eyes got big. "He exposed himself in public? I checked him for priors, but he didn't have any."

"The judge let him go with a warning. Didn't even get a mark on his record."

"I wish there were a way I could get that little seed of information to the jury."

"Seed? Very funny." Tai tapped the disk with his finger. "But I got something much better. Reread his police interview, then watch this. You won't be sorry." He picked up his tray and left.

Summer looked at the title scrawled on the label: *Kinky Ninja Sex Girls*. She left her breakfast partially eaten and headed upstairs to view it.

———————

Rhonda Spellman, Gundy's building superintendent, took the stand. She was a gray, wrinkly woman with a stooped spine from years of mopping, sweeping, and providing maintenance to Gundy's fellow condo dwellers. She had dressed up for her moment in the sun, wearing a dress and shoes too modern for her Old World figure. Her hands were leathery, but that hadn't stopped her from getting a manicure. During Raines's direct, she peppered her testimony with polite gestures: "Yes, sir" and "No, sir" and "I really couldn't say, Mr. Raines."

Spellman said she had encountered "a pretty, redheaded woman" on the condo complex premises the morning of the murder. She didn't know how old the woman was. Everyone under 50 all looked alike to her, she said. Her testimony culminated with Raines asking her to identify the woman with whom she had spoken.

Without pause, she pointed to SK.

Summer smiled as she approached the witness stand. She could easily impeach Spellman's credibility—in her interview with Tai, she had said she wore glasses but couldn't recall whether she'd been wearing them when she encountered SK. But rattling Spellman would only upset the jury. Besides, Summer needed to explain SK's fingerprints on the crime photos and on the door.

"Did Ms. Killington seem angry when you saw her?" Summer asked.

"No, ma'am," she said. "Seemed real nice. I said 'Nice weather' and she smiled and said, 'Yes, it is.' Then, 'Have yourself a real nice day.' These days not too many people are that friendly."

"That does sound friendly. Did she try to hide from you?"

"Oh, no, ma'am."

"Didn't try to skulk around the back way, right?"

"No, ma'am."

"You didn't see her any other time did you?"

"No, I didn't. Just the once."

"Not that evening."

"No."

"Did you see where she went after you talked with her?"

"No, ma'am, I didn't," Spellman said. "I had a lot of work to do."

"Was she carrying anything?"

Spellman offered Summer an exaggerated shrug. "Couldn't say one way or the other. I remember what she looked like, but after that, I really wasn't paying much attention."

"No further questions, Your Honor," Summer said. "And Mrs. Spellman, you have yourself a real nice day."

Spellman nodded. "You too, dearie."

After Summer sat down at the defense table, SK tapped her knee.

"Good job," she said.

But Summer knew she had blundered. She had committed a cardinal sin for defense attorneys: asking a question she didn't already know the answer to. Spellman hadn't seen SK leave the photos at Gundy's door. Although it was possible the jury would conclude there was a good chance that SK had left them to remind of Gundy of an egregious error in judgment, it was far more likely they would believe that SK had been casing his condo with plans to return later.

Summer may have inadvertently characterized SK as the merry murderer.

She glanced at Raines, who was smirking at her.

Next in line was Malcolm Byers, a 25-year old local with a life going nowhere fast. He testified that he had been delivering two stuffed-crust pizzas with mushrooms to one of Gundy's neighbors at the time of the murder.

Byers was pimply and awkward, his hair scraggly, his clothes ill-fitting. Raines led him through his testimony. He claimed he'd seen a "skinny redheaded woman" in black leather tights and a snug halter top run from Gundy's at 10:10 p.m. "That woman," he said, pointing at SK.

"You saw her open the door of Mr. Gundy's condo?" Raines asked.

"Hell, yeah," Byers said.

"What did you see?"

"The defendant all sweaty, like she'd been working out real hard. She poked her head out to make sure no one was around, but since I was coming out of the house across the way, and I was in the dark, she couldn't see me."

"What else, Mr. Byers?"

"I saw her do this weird kung fu action, like, move her hands like this." Byers curled his elbows in and waved his hands threateningly, accompanying it with a squawk. "Something like that," he said.

Summer had to shush SK.

"And then?" Raines asked.

Byers's face lit up. "Oh, yeah, man, it was so cool. She ran off and just before she got to this fence she did this awesome handspring and fuckin'—sorry—leaped over the fence. I was scared, 'cause a woman like that could kill you."

"You said she was moving quickly; but did you, perchance, notice what she was wearing on her feet?" Raines asked.

"Boots," Byers said. "She was pretty still when she first left the condo, so I got a real good look."

Raines held up Exhibit 27B, the boots that Tyler had testified were the ones he'd found at SK's. "Do you recognize these as the boots she was wearing?"

Byers nodded yes.

"Let the record indicate that Mr. Byers is nodding his head in agreement," Raines said.

"Got me a pair just like them at home," Byers added. "St. Croix brand. Good for stomping people, if, that's, like, what you're into."

Summer was so eager to begin her cross-examination that on her way to greet Byers she stumbled. She took Byers through past run-ins with teachers and principals in high school and the jobs he was fired from for stealing or flunking lie detector tests.

When Summer asked about his taste in movies, Raines objected. "What does that have to do with anything?" he asked.

"If the court will bear with me for a moment," Summer said.

The judge looked down imperiously. "A very brief moment, Counselor."

"Yes, Your Honor," she responded. "Now, Mr. Byers, what films do you like to watch?"

Byers shifted in the chair. "All kinds."

"Do you ever rent movies from a store?"

"Yeah. From Smitties Video on Allen Street."

"Do you ever rent pornographic DVDs?"

Byers looked like he had been shot. "Maybe."

To make him sweat, Summer took her time walking over to the defense table. She picked up a pile of printouts: a record of every title Byers had rented over the last three years. She handed a set to Raines.

"Maybe?" Summer repeated.

"Sometimes," Byers said.

Raines, after skimming the list, jumped up. "Objection. I fail to see what relevance any of this has to this case."

"Judge," Summer said, "May I have a word with you and Mr. Raines in chambers?"

Hightower leaned back in his chair and consulted the clock. "All right. Let's take a 20-minute break. Ms. Neuwirth, Mr. Raines, give me a couple of minutes, then join me in chambers."

Raines was already inside when Summer arrived. Hightower was on a step stool, tossing books into a box. Judging by the tension in the air, it was apparent that the two of them were not speaking. The election was only ten days away. Although he clearly held Raines in disdain, as far as Summer could tell, thus far Hightower hadn't let this influence him.

"Have a seat, Summer," Hightower said. "You don't mind if I continue to clean up a bit while we discuss this, do you?"

Do I have a choice? she thought. "Of course not, Your Honor."

Hightower dropped more books into the box. "Legal thrillers my wife gave me. She's quite a fan."

Summer reached into the box and pulled out a bestseller called *Primal Evidence*. She read the back: *The improbable story of a schizophrenic alcoholic who solves the murder of a child actress and inadvertently stumbles onto an international conspiracy involving the Catholic church.*

"Actually," Hightower said, taking the book from Summer and flipping through it, "this one was kind of good. I heard it's going to be the big movie at Christmas this year."

Raines said, "Can we get down to business?"

With a meaty sigh, Hightower stepped down and took his place behind his desk. "Now, why did you request this meeting, Summer?"

"I have here a list of every DVD Mr. Byers rented from Smitties over the past year," she said. "Out of more than 200 of them, 129 of them were porno movies, many of them rented repeatedly."

"So?" Raines asked.

"Did you corner the market in moral impropriety?" Summer asked. "You dredged up a 20-year old prostitution conviction."

"That's different. One is a conviction and the other is—" Raines shut up when Hightower held up his hand.

"Surely you have more to offer me than Mr. Byers's lust for pornography," Hightower said.

"Yes, sir," Summer said. "I have here a DVD that Mr. Byers rented nine times, a porno flick called, excuse my French, *Kinky Ninja Sex Girls*. May I play a section of it for you?"

Raines snorted, "Judge, you can't be entertaining the notion that I, or the jury for the matter, has to be subjected to this filth."

"The scene in question has no nudity," Summer said, "and it's brief. Your Honor, I believe you have an obligation to at least view the segment I have marked."

"This better not be a waste of my time." Hightower took the disc from Summer and slid it into his DVD player.

Afterward, he said, "I have no choice but to allow this to be entered into evidence."

Summer cued up the scene and Sprague hit "play" on the judge's command. While Byers and the jury watched on a monitor, a man and woman engaged in combat, complete with fists of fury and hokey sound effects. The woman, a ninja assassin dressed in black leather tights and a halter top, kicked the man in the face. He was knocked to the ground. She straddled him as he begged for mercy and snapped his neck cleanly.

Cat-like, she made her way to the door. She peeked once left, then right. After quietly shutting the door behind her, she darted into the night. Just before coming upon a tall chain link fence, she performed a handspring and vaulted over it, disappearing into the night.

PART V

INFOMANIA

CHAPTER 28

"I'VE WORKED FOR THE public defenders office for more than 20 years and I've never had anything like that happen to me," Levi said. "How did you ever find that DVD?"

Summer was in Levi's office, reclining on his couch while Levi had his shoes off and his feet up on his desk. His air conditioner hissed, leaked water, and groaned. Levi said he thought of it as a house pet. A vinyl record spun on a turntable playing 60s rock, complete with pops and hiss, which Levi claimed added to the ambience.

"It's all Tai's handiwork," Summer said.

"And you didn't want him."

"I was dead wrong." Summer massaged her bare heel. "I know this is a little immoral, but I'm hoping the jury relives this moment over and over again via the media. Maybe it'll have a cumulative effect, encourage them to vote 'not guilty.' Sure, they all promise when they're selected that they won't read newspaper, magazine, or television accounts of the trial, but how can they not overhear something on TV or glimpse a headline?"

"That's a perfectly normal desire, as long as you don't foster it. But don't rely on it. The D.A.'s won cases with a lot less evidence than this, so keep up the pressure. I assume you're going to rest without mounting a defense."

"You betcha," she said, "although SK is making noise like she wants to testify; she wants to use the witness stand as a pulpit. I've avoided committing to this in the hopes she'll see that we're way up on points, and that the best strategy would be to shut up until after the trial. Then, let her write a book for all I care."

"Sound judgment." Levi itched one foot with the toes of his other, which poked through a hole. "You know, this is your lucky day for another reason. I just got a call from Jimi Cruz."

Summer heard sounds of shock come out of her mouth, finally managing, "I thought he was dead"; then immediately regretted saying it.

But it was too oblique a reference for Levi to catch. "Dead? Well, the way he was going, I can see why you'd think that. He called to say he got a slot in a local drug rehab program and wanted me to thank you. Let's face it: If it wasn't for you, he'd be in the slammer for 25 to life calling some 300-pound goon named Bubba 'Honey.' "

If Cruz wasn't dead, then what other pieces of information had Marsalis toyed with? She had to fight the urge to deconstruct every moment she had suffered through with him, but she had ten minutes to get back to court.

It would have to wait.

Summer ran into Rosie on her way out. Together they walked down the concrete steps in front of the building and out to the boulevard, where they waited at the stoplight.

"*Kinky Ninja Sex Girls*?" Rosie's tongue was pushed against her cheek. "It's all over the court building."

Summer tossed her head back. "If Raines had a streak of decency, he'd move to dismiss, but with the election coming up, and the fact that he's a sanctimonious pain in the ass, he'll take his chances with a jury."

The light changed and they crossed through the car exhaust.

"Did you tell Jon about, you know, the gang thing?" Rosie asked.

"If he ever finds out, it'll have to come from you."

"Thanks."

"Don't thank me. Everybody has nasty little secrets. Maybe if I had a stronger character or a better sense of what was right or wrong, I'd dissolve our friendship. But given the fact that 98 percent of the clients we represent are guilty, I'd be a hypocrite if I did. Besides, The Latin Brothers play rough. If I were in your shoes, I don't know what I'd do either. And I wouldn't want anything to happen to you."

Before Summer entered the court building, Rosie chucked her in the arm. "With a little luck, SK will be out in time for the weekend," she said.

When court convened, Summer found that it would take more than a little luck. While the jury waited inside the deliberation room, Raines announced that he had come across new evidence in the last 24 hours.

"A witness," he said.

"Your Honor, it's a little late in the game to be dumping a surprise witness on us," Summer said. "What is the nature of this witness's testimony?"

"Well, Mr. Raines," Hightower asked.

Raines strode confidently. "The nature of her testimony is that Ms. Killington has killed before."

Summer quickly whispered to SK, "Do you know what this is about?"

SK was ashen. "I think so. And if I'm right, I'm dead."

Hightower agreed to hear the witness, and the jury was brought in. Nurse Patti Dowden, a middle-aged woman with timid hair, a heavy bosom, and the wisp of an Irish brogue took the stand. Raines told her to recount what she had told the D.A.'s office the day before.

"Three years ago, I was working the night shift at County Hospital when a man was brought in," she said. "He had several broken bones, internal injuries, and a ruptured spleen. He was rushed into surgery and operated on for four hours. But the man died the next day."

"What was his name?"

Dowden answered so softly the judge had to remind her to speak up. "Lawrence Bishop." She rolled the 'r' in *Lawrence*.

"You testified that this happened three years ago, and, although so many patients pass through your hospital, you say you remember his name. Why?"

"His story was so unbelievable and the circumstances so frightening, I could not forget."

She had the kind of voice you could trust. Summer frantically searched for a strategy.

"What did he tell you?" Raines asked.

The jury was mesmerized. Summer considered objecting, claim it was hearsay, but she knew Raines would counter that it was a deathbed confession. Better to hear it out now.

"He told me he attacked a woman who was walking across

the park late at night. He said he was carrying a knife, and when he saw her, he intended to rape her."

"So what happened?"

"He jumped her from behind, but was not prepared for the fact that the woman could defend herself. She disarmed him, kicked him in the groin, and when he was down, beat him badly."

"How badly did this woman beat Mr. Bishop?"

"She had broken both his arms, dislocated his shoulder, ruptured his spleen, fractured several of his ribs, and crushed his testicles. I know what he did was wrong, but noth—"

"Object— No, no, I withdraw it." Summer was just making it worse. Raines had been crafty. He hadn't even mentioned SK.

Raines smiled at the jury, and then turned to Dowden. "You were saying."

"Nothing justifies what happened to him."

Raines entered the hospital record and Bishop's death certificate into evidence. Then he asked, "When Mr. Bishop was fighting for his life, who called for the ambulance?"

"Mr. Bishop did. The woman dragged him to a pay telephone, dialed 9-1-1, and let the receiver hang down."

Raines played the 9-1-1 tape. The voice of a dispatcher. "Police. State the nature of your emergency."

A man's groans in the distance. He must have been a foot away from the receiver. "Help," he gasped.

"Sir, where are you?"

He sobbed. "I've been beaten."

"Where are you?" the dispatcher repeated.

"H-help."

The dispatcher screamed, "*Where are you?*"

"P-p-park." Then a long rattle. Silence.

"*Sir? Sir?!*" But no response.

"After surgery, did Mr. Bishop ever regain consciousness?" Raines asked Dowden.

"Yes."

Raines paced away from the witness stand. "Did Mr. Bishop identify the woman who did this to him?"

"Yes, he did. He told me it was the director of the Women's Center, located a couple blocks south of the park."

Summer saw an opening. Dowden hadn't specifically identified SK. It was a long shot but worth pursuing.

Until Dowden dropped the next bomb.

"A few hours after Mr. Bishop died, she"—Dowden pointed to SK—"came to the hospital."

"Let the record reflect that the witness pointed to the defendant," Raines said. "Did she tell you why she came?"

"Yes. She told me she'd been attacked by a man in the park and wanted to know how he was faring."

"What did you say?"

"I told her the man had died."

"What did she say?"

"'Too bad.' Then she left the hospital."

"That's it?" Raines said in a voice tinged with disapproval. "*Too bad?* A man is dead, and that's all she said?"

"Yes."

"Your witness," Raines said to Summer.

But he was wrong about that. Dowden was definitely Raines's witness.

<hr />

After court had recessed for the weekend, Summer strode into the holding cell. SK was lying face down on the bench.

"Why didn't you tell me about this?" Summer yelled.

"I'd almost forgotten about it," SK said without looking up. "He attacked me. He tried to rape me. Was I supposed to let him get away with it?"

"You killed him."

"I defended myself. Wouldn't you love to kill the man who raped you?" SK rolled onto her back. "What do we do now?"

Summer slowly ran her hand down her face. "I don't know."

"Well, maybe our luck will change when I take the stand," SK said.

Summer sputtered. "No way you're getting on that stand."

SK scrambled up and approached the bars. "Yes, I am."

"I know what you're thinking. You want to get up there and use it as a soapbox. You want to attack the police, the D.A., the system. But all you'll do is make things worse."

"Can things get any worse?"

"A lot worse."

"I'm not budging on this, Summer. You've done a great job, but it looks like Raines got lucky. All right. So I'm going down. But I'm not going to just sit there and let it happen without a fight."

"Don't do it, SK. Give me a chance to finish this. Let me do it the way I think it should be done."

SK took a deep breath, sniffled, and shut her eyes. When she opened them, Summer saw they were teary. "I know I didn't treat you with respect when I first met you, but over time I've come to really appreciate you. You're a great attorney and I'm lucky to have you. The weird thing is, it's like I've always known you. There's this odd connection I feel to you—like we're family."

SK returned to the bench and flopped down.

"Give me the weekend to think of something," Summer said, blinking. "If I can't come up with a plan of action, it's your call whether you take the stand or not."

CHAPTER 29

SUMMER WAS RAGING INSIDE. *So close,* she thought. *So close to pulling this off.* But now it looked like she had lost; and worse, SK would end up on death row, where she would spend her remaining years fighting for an appeal, then clemency, then a stay of execution, until the day the jail doctor would shoot an IV drip into her arm and poison would spread into her blood.

She fumbled with her house keys, turning each one, lock by lock, only vaguely aware of the crystal breeze and pounding surf behind her, the sky limned by darkening clouds, the seagulls circling above, calling, swooping.

When she turned the knob, she was grabbed from behind. A silvery blade squeezed her windpipe. Summer heard the ratchety sound of duct tape being unraveled from its roll.

She squeezed her assailant's pinky and twisted it, trying to snap the joint. She swung her other arm straight up and back, striking her attacker's head. The knife clattered to the deck.

She whirled and aimed for his groin.

But Marsalis dodged her kicks. He cupped two fists together, wound up, and hit her. Summer felt the impact explode inside her head. She crumpled to the ground. Marsalis pushed the door open and dragged her inside by her hair. He stepped outside and retrieved the knife.

Summer screamed, but only the rumbling surf could hear.

He kicked the door closed and bolted the locks. Summer was groggy. She tried to get up, but Marsalis fell on her chest, pinning her. He bit off a strip of duct tape.

Summer watched as Marsalis pushed the tape down toward her eyes. She brought her knee up in desperation and caught him from underneath. Marsalis winced as all the air escaped from his lungs.

Summer tried to knee him again, but he turned sideways and rolled off her, his body ending up flush against the door. He was curled up in a ball, crying without tears, the knife still in his hands.

She raced to her closet to look for the gun Wib had given her. She swung the door open and began rummaging. She heard Marsalis stumble to his feet. He picked up a chair and threw it, smashing it into her back and forcing the air out of her lungs. She fell to the floor, gasping.

Marsalis, too, had fallen on all fours. He clenched the knife in his teeth and crawled toward her. "Much better this time, Summer," he said through tight teeth. "I must commend you for learning from your past mistakes."

"You bastard."

He stopped crawling and sat still, clutching himself. "I was merely recreating one of the more memorable moments of your life."

"How long have you been stalking me Marsalis? From the time I was raped? That was more than six months ago."

"Longer."

"Did you kill Sonia?"

"She killed herself."

"But you helped?"

"I shared with her my knowledge about the circumstances surrounding her child's death and your subsequent illegal adoption. She was dying anyway. It appears that she was seeking a convenient rationale to end the pain of cancer."

"Perhaps," Summer conceded.

"Now, I am willing to tell you who your real mother is—for a price."

"Your information is not to be trusted," Summer said. "In fact, you've waged a campaign of misinformation. Jimi Cruz, for example."

"That was for sheer irritainment value." He removed the knife from his mouth and showed it to her. "Surely this must indicate that I have the goods. Does it look familiar?"

Summer ran through escape options. Marsalis was between her and the locked front door. There was no back exit, and the windows were securely fastened. In her zeal to keep out intruders, she had effectively trapped herself. "Is that the same knife used to burn my back?"

"A replica. But since you were blindfolded, I assume you did not get a good look." He licked the blade and made a sizzling sound.

"Did you rape Davenport just so you would end up with me as your attorney?"

"If I hadn't wished to get caught, I would have killed her. And I certainly would not have sent her the video."

Then it all clicked for Summer. "Your mother didn't just disappear."

Marsalis threw the knife into the floor where it stuck blade first. "Bravo, Summer."

"How could you kill your own mother?"

"She was a very naughty girl," Marsalis said. "She had me out of wedlock when she was 18. She hated me for robbing her of her youth. I grew up alone in my room. She wouldn't allow me to leave for days, weeks sometimes. I realized the only way I would ever be able to taste freedom was to take hers. But it wasn't until I was 15 that I was able to work up the courage. After one of her flings left her bedroom, I tied her up and executed her with a knife—a knife not dissimilar to this one. Afterwards, I buried her in the hills. The body was never found."

"There's one detail you haven't told me. You weren't an only child."

"Yes."

"A sister, right?"

"Yes. A sister who my mother treated like a princess while I was locked inside my room."

Summer felt a pain shoot through her heart. She could feel fear jangle every nerve ending. "Now you've come to complete your job as executioner."

"It must be this way. Unfortunately, my mother lived in pre-Internet times. She's gone forever. But now, I can relive that moment of total freedom and euphoria whenever I wish—forever. Right after I fuck you, Sister, I'm going to kill you, then share it with the world over the Internet. Summer and Shadow—don't you see?"

"Why didn't you kill me the first time you met me?"

"I had to be sure you were who I thought you were. I also

wished to become reacquainted with you. It *had* been a long time."

"How did you find me?"

"I searched for you for ten years. Why do you think I became an information broker in the first place?" Marsalis scrambled to his feet. "It's time."

"Wait!" Summer tried to buy time. "I still don't understand why you put Gundy under surveillance."

Marsalis laughed. "Of course you do, Summer. He hurt you. I couldn't allow him to get away with that."

He moved a step closer.

Summer backed away until her back was pressed firmly against her desk, where her computer sat. She put up her hands in self-defense and stared at the blade tip as it homed in on her face.

A look of ecstasy crossed Marsalis's face. Moaning softly, he lowered the blade to her chest and flicked off the top button of her blouse with the tip. Then he started on the second.

"This is a glorious moment," he said.

CHAPTER 30

JUDGE HIGHTOWER WAS PACING HIS CHAMBERS and anxiously tugging on his robe.

"What a mess," he said. "What a fucking, unadulterated mess. What's the ME say about all of this?"

Chantelle was bleary-eyed and her clothes looked like they had been balled up and unfurled. "I ran some preliminary tests, and I cannot say with any certainty that it is not the same killer. The victim died in the same manner as Mr. Gundy. Toxicology tests are not in yet, but I did get a good whiff of mescal, or perhaps tequila. And there is the same odd mark on the back, too. This wasn't publicized, was it?"

Detective Tyler shook his head. "We kept it from the press to discourage copycats, although I suppose someone here in the court system could have gotten wind."

Hightower said, "It didn't even come up during the trial. Why is that, Mr. Raines?"

"The prosecution contends the mark was a red herring,

that the defendant was trying to throw the police off her trail," Raines said. "That's why we didn't bother having that aspect of the ME's report entered into the record. Since the defense hasn't presented its case yet, it's obvious why we didn't hear it from them."

"Do you wish to amend that contention?" Hightower asked.

"No," Raines answered. "I'm not convinced it's the same murderer. The physical evidence is, for now, inconclusive. And there are key differences. Namely, that the body was dumped on the courthouse steps sometime during the night. There is no evidence that the victim was killed at home like the others. Also, the victim is obviously not in law enforcement."

Hightower tweaked his venetian blinds and looked out on the swarm of media out front. "So what are we going to do about this case? The national media's gotten hold of it. Already my court clerk has received hundreds of calls and thousands of emails begging me to drop the charges."

Raines looked out the window. "How do we know the jury's not tainted?"

Hightower sipped bourbon. It was early, but... "As soon as I got the word, I told the bailiffs to round them up and sequester them, but they could have gotten an earful of media coverage on this. They couldn't have known to shut off their TVs, radios, and not read the newspapers. They were told to avoid the Stephanie Killington case. I interviewed each one independently; most of them admitted they'd heard about this latest murder but swore they'd be able to reach a fair and impartial verdict."

"The question is, can we believe them?" Raines asked. "They've invested more than a week into this trial. My experience with jurors is once they've been seated, they want to go the distance. How do we know they're not telling you what you want to hear?"

"You make a valid point, but what do you want me to do—declare a mistrial? Wait for the police to complete their investigation?"

"Absolutely not."

The judge went to the window again and fiddled with the blinds. After surveying the press corps again, he focused his eyes on Raines. "There is another option available to us."

Raines stood, pushing his chair back with the backs of his legs. "I won't do it. There is no way I'll drop the charges."

"If I declare a mistrial, there's no way you'll win next time around and you know it," Hightower shot back. "Your eyewitness is a kook, your physical evidence is shit, and there is substantial proof that Detective Tyler planted evidence."

Tyler opened his mouth to speak, but thought better of it.

"If I let the jury decide," Hightower continued, "there's a good chance they'll acquit Ms. Killington anyway. There's no way that at least one of them wasn't influenced by the similarities in these two murders. Frankly, if I were on the jury, I'd vote to acquit her because you did not present compelling proof of her guilt."

"If you're so sure," Raines said, "then why don't you tell the jury to go home and issue a directed verdict of not guilty?"

Hightower smiled sweetly. "That's a marvelous suggestion."

Raines chewed on his bottom lip, his dreams of a judgeship in tatters. He took a moment to weigh his options. "The D.A. drops the charges."

"Even better," the judge said, barely able to conceal his glee.

Raines kicked the wastebasket on his way out, scattering balls of paper and tissues.

After Raines slammed the door behind him, Hightower calmly bent down to pick up the mess. When he was finished, he turned his attention to the back of the room.

"Summer," he said, "Please extend my apologies to your client about this miscarriage of justice. I'm afraid Mr. Raines was a little too ambitious."

Summer had been seated quietly, fidgeting with her turtleneck. Thankfully the weather was cooler today. "I will, Judge."

"Good." Hightower stood over her. "I must point out that two out of four of the main players in the Marsalis video-rape trial are now dead. I have accepted the police's offer of protection and recommend you do too until they get to the bottom of this."

"No police protection for me, Your Honor," she said simply.

"Have it your way, Summer."

EPILOGUE

SUMMER DUG THROUGH HER CLOSET and removed a garbage bag. She dumped the contents on the floor. The window looking out on to the sea was boarded up. There was a patch of dried blood not far from the desk where she had once kept her computer.

Clack-clack-clack at the door. "It's Tai. Open up."

Summer was too weary to move. "Door's open."

Tai came in, his arm wrapped in gauze and supported by a sling. He surveyed the mess. "We have to get rid of this stuff," he said.

"Well, things were tight." Summer looked up at him. "It's hard for me to trust anyone. Things may not always be smooth between us."

He touched her cheek with his good hand. "I know. Besides, you're a killer and I'm an accomplice to jury tampering."

"And about a dozen other violations of the penal code." Summer looked into his eyes and lost herself in their sparkling green. "I'll never be able to thank you for saving my life. When Marsalis held that knife at my throat, I saw my whole life flash before my eyes, and not only was it a short reel, I didn't like what I saw."

"You saved my life too, don't you remember?" Tai mussed her hair. "You know when I figured it out?"

Summer began putting the tape, gun, condoms, and knife back into the bag and waited for Tai to continue.

"At my place," Tai said, "after you told me about the scars on your back. Ignacio told me a similar story of sado-masochistic kink after I sprung her."

"Why didn't you tell me?"

Tai looked at her like she was as dense as the language in the penal code. "I didn't want to scare you off. Besides, if you denied it, what was I going to do? Without you, your client would have fried for a murder she didn't commit. I got no problem how this turned out: Gundy deserved to die. In cop talk, we say it's a 'C.C.'—'condition corrected.' "

"Can't argue with that."

"But to satisfy my curiosity... tell me what happened the night Gundy died?"

Summer twisted the end of the bag and tied it in a knot. "I didn't go over there with the intent to hurt him. I just wanted to find proof that he was the one who raped me. I held a gun on him and made him tell me where he kept his tools. Gundy was a coward. He was easy to intimidate. I made him pull his pants down and stand by the railing on the second floor so I could keep my eye on him while I searched his bedroom closet. After I found this garbage bag and all his neat little toys inside, I started to call the police, but he freaked. He knew I couldn't just shoot him, so he hopped toward me and grabbed the gun. We fought over it. He lost his balance, tripped, and crashed through the railing." Summer stopped to take a deep breath, living in the memory.

Tai prodded gently. "And then?"

Her voice wavered. "He was in bad shape when I got to him. I didn't know what to do. He started to dial 9-1-1, but he died before completing the call. I realized this was a point of no return: He was the highest-ranking prosecutor in the county, and I just knew the D.A. would find a way to string me up. Then I remembered that old case my father worked on; hence the mescal and lipstick."

"Strickland," Tai said.

"Strickland," Summer repeated. "But two things went wrong. Number one, I forgot about the pictures of Jonathan Sadbury. They just didn't seem important at the time. When the cops arrested SK and I was appointed to represent her, I almost turned myself in. But that would have meant that Gundy would not only have succeeded in scarring me for life, but getting me thrown in jail, too. I just couldn't let him win."

"And number two was Marsalis."

Summer nodded. "He had video of me in Gundy's apartment when he died."

"That's why you wouldn't let the cops—or me, for that matter—help you out," Tai said. "What tipped you off about Gundy?"

"After one heated exchange during Marsalis's rape trial, he and I had words in the elevator. 'How do you know you're not defending your rapist?' he asked. 'How do you know he isn't the one who burned your back?' But the thing is, not a soul could have known about that. I was too ashamed to tell anyone."

Tai whistled through his teeth. "Aren't you afraid someone's going to stumble on to Marsalis's website and find that video of you killing Gundy?"

"No," she said. "This website will always be up, floating around in cyberland, but accessible only to me, since I'm the only one who knows the passwords. If anyone ever finds Marsalis's hideaway, and I wouldn't bet on it, it'll set off an alarm and cut off access, like it did when the cops found his surveillance equipment at Gundy's condo. If someone tries to hack in with the wrong passwords, the site will either implode, or, knowing Marsalis, it'll send out a nasty virus. I think what's really weird is that Marsalis wanted his final attack on me to be immortalized on the Internet. Ironically, it will be, only I'm the only one able to access it."

"Forget about Gundy," Tai said. "I want to see us."

Summer clicked on the icon labeled "Summer's House" and scrolled to a date two days prior. She double-clicked on it and the screen blossomed into video. Summer fast-forwarded past the point where Marsalis dragged her inside by her hair, past the fight and conversation, up until the point where he was plucking buttons off her blouse one at a time with his knife.

While the computer whirred, Summer and Tai watched intently:

> *Marsalis dug the blade into her neck and pulled up her skirt, his hand crawling upward. "Let your fingers do the walking," he sang.*
>
> *"Marsalis, stop it!" She punched him square in the face.*
>
> *He stopped for an instant, and then curled his hand and squeezed.*
>
> *Summer cried out.*
>
> *He cut Summer's bra off with the knife and her breasts fell free.*

Marsalis bent over to lick them, when there was a shattering explosion of glass.

Tai was writhing on the floor, rolling in glass, yelling, "Shit, shit, shit!" His gun had been jarred from his hand.

Marsalis let go of Summer and turned on him. Before Tai could retrieve the gun, Marsalis raised the knife like a javelin and threw it. The blade pierced Tai's arm and pinned him to the floor. Tai screamed. Blood flowed out of him.

The gun was just precious inches out of his grasp. When he couldn't reach it, Tai fought through the pain and struggled to unpin himself. Marsalis approached, and Tai wrestled with the knife and, while roaring in agony, yanked it out of his arm.

Marsalis, calculating the distance, turned back from Tai, who was fumbling with the gun safety, and pulled out the plugs inputted into Summer's computer monitor. He picked it up over his head and started toward Tai, who was operating with only one hand, his bad one.

Marsalis was about to heave the computer when Summer leaped up and kicked him from behind. Marsalis's spine buckled. He lost his balance, slipping on Tai's blood. The computer came crashing down on his head. Marsalis was still, his legs bent, his arms spread out.

Summer ran to Tai, who was covered in sticky blood. She told him she would be right back and returned with a towel. She made a tourniquet for him.

"What do we do about him?" Tai asked.

"I suppose I should check his pulse, see if he's alive."

"Don't." Tai grunted his way to his feet. He winced. *"You got any booze?"*

"Under the kitchen sink."

Tai, holding his arm up, fetched a bottle of tequila. He handed it to Summer. "Could you open it?"

She did and Tai took two deep sips. He sighed. "That's better." He handed the bottle back to her. "Put the cap back on, please." She did. "Now, wipe the bottle thoroughly with your shirt."

"What are you going to do?"

"Get SK off, that's what I'm going to do."

Summer shut the computer down.

Tai touched the tender part of his arm. "What now?" he asked.

"I think it's up to you," Summer said.

Tai extracted a pair of handcuffs from his blazer pocket. One shackle he cuffed to her wrist, the other to his.

Summer didn't resist. "You're arresting me?"

Tai led her to the bedroom and pulled her on to the bed. "Who said anything about arresting you?" he said. "I'm just making sure you don't run away again."

He unknotted the sling and tossed it aside, then pushed her shoulders down onto the bed, until she was pinned under him.

Between kisses, he said, "Hang on, Summer, because I'm going to love you today, tomorrow, forever."

THE END

ABOUT THE
AUTHOR

Adam L. Penenberg is a journalism professor at New York University who has written for *Fast Company*, *Forbes*, the *New York Times*, the *Washington Post*, *Wired*, *Slate*, *Playboy*, and the *Economist*. A former senior editor at *Forbes* and a reporter for Forbes.com, Penenberg garnered national attention in 1998 for unmasking serial fabricator Stephen Glass of the *New Republic*. Penenberg's story was a watershed for online investigative journalism and portrayed in the film *Shattered Glass* (Steve Zahn plays Penenberg).

Penenberg has published several books that have been optioned for film and serialized in the *New York Times Magazine*, *Wired UK*, and the *Financial Times*, and won a Deadline Club Award for feature reporting for his *Fast Company* story "Revenge of the Nerds," which looked at the future of moviemaking. He has appeared on NBC's *The Today Show* as well as on CNN and all the major news networks, and has been quoted about media and technology in the *Washington Post*, the *Christian Science Monitor*, *USA Today*, *Wired News*, *Ad Age*, *Marketwatch*, *Politico*, and many others.

Wayzgoose Press is proud to present Adam's novel
Virtually True:

True Ailey is a journalist in a strange land, exiled by his network to a damp Southeast Asian republic gouged out a war-ravaged peninsula weeping monsoon tears. When his friend is murdered, True sets out to find the killers, and in the process untangles a vast conspiracy that threatens to upend the global balance of power. Set in the near future, *Virtually True* takes readers on a wild ride through a world where nothing is what it seems, corporations rule, technology has been woven into the fabric of people's lives, and information can be both weapon and life-saver.

Award-winning journalist Adam Penenberg, whom *Slate* called "one of the best-known technology writers in the world," has peopled a literary thriller with unforgettable characters and crafted a plot worthy of Philip K. Dick, William Gibson, and Martin Cruz Smith.